RIVERS

BOOK 3
UNKNOWN TRAILS

MIKE DILLINGHAM

Publication Consultants — Since 1978

PO Box 221974 Anchorage, Alaska 99522-1974
books@publicationconsultants.com—www.publicationconsultants.com

ISBN 978-1-59433-082-7

Library of Congress Catalog Card Number: 2008933964

Other books by Mike Dillingham
Rivers, Diary of a Blind Alaska Racing Sled Dog
Rivers, Through the Eyes of a Blind Dog

Manufactured in the United States of America.

High Gang, Rivers Here!

Contents

Photo Credits

All pictures in this book except for the pictures on the front and back covers, the "Hi Gang Rivers here" and See ya" pages come from the personal collection of the author of Rivers Books © 2008. The front and rear cover pictures, as well as those listed above, plus the photos on the "Hi Gang Rivers Here" and "See Ya" pages are used with permission of Donna Quante of Husky Productions © 2008. The picture of Sandy Quandt and Rivers on the "Forward" page, Lakota's picture on the "Cast of Critters" page as well as the picture of Mary and I on the "Acknowledgments" page come from Sandy and Tony Quandt's private collection and are used with their permission. The pictures of Stormy (Stryker in the book) and Ron Aiello are from the personal collection of Ronald L. Aiello, President of the United States War Dog Association, and are used with his permission.

Cast of Critters

Rivers

Lakota

Christmas

Tundra

Sky

Stormy

Brownie

Nitro

Doc

Fin

Ugly

Sunny

Sandy

Stryker

Geezer

Foreword

My friendship with Rivers began the first year I used *Rivers, Diary of a Blind Alaska Racing Sled Dog* as a read-aloud to my class of fourth graders in Seabrook, Texas. My students gained more from listening to Rivers' adventures than getting out of work, and hearing a nice dog story. My students gained valuable life lessons, as well.

Timeless words of wisdom ran through each of the first two Rivers books, and *Rivers Book 3, Unknown Trails* does not disappoint in continuing that tradition. Themes of confronting challenges, not giving up, overcoming those challenges, and doing your best, are integral to the telling of Rivers' stories. Each of us can learn much from Rivers and his pals, both canine and human. Compassion for those in need, the importance of family and friends and  cherishing, instead of taking for granted, those around you, are also lessons reaped from these pages.

These enduring qualities lie woven inside a story filled with adventure, emotion, and intrigue. In *Rivers Book 3*, Lakota relates to Rivers what Mike has just asked Stryker. "Well, Buddy, do you want to stay with us? Do you want to join our team?"

I ask you the same question. Do you want to stay with Rivers and join the team? You will be glad you said, "Yes."

Sandy Quandt
Educator
Space Academy for Educators Alumni, U.S. Space Camp

Old Geezer

Some nights you just cannot sleep. This was one of those nights. There was nothing on my mind to keep me awake. However, my instincts told me I should get up and walk around the yard. I did not know what time it was since dogs do not tell time. It was a cool night, with a soft whisper of a breeze playing around my ears. I heard the sounds of my buddies snoring as they slumbered in their doghouses.

As I wandered around the yard, I heard paw steps coming towards me from two different directions. The paw steps behind me would belong to Stormy. She has taken on the role of my "eyes", and has this uncanny knack of knowing when I am up and where I am.

She was about to say something when I asked her to keep silent. I wanted to focus on the other set of paw steps. We walked in the direction of those paw steps. They were coming up the driveway that is next to the big house.

The paw steps were very soft and slow. I told Stormy that I bet an older dog, or a dog who is not well, is walking towards us. I asked her if she could see anything. Stormy said she could not and asked if she should wake the other dogs.

"No," I replied. "This dog is not a threat to us."

When we reached the gate, we stopped, and waited before I softly barked, "Hello. Is anyone there?"

The steps stopped and there was silence. Again, I barked, "Hello, is anyone there?" I sensed Stormy going into her defensive mode as she moved closer to me.

"Easy Stormy," I said. "This dog is not a threat to us."

"That may be true, Uncle Rivers," Stormy replied. "But the dog has not answered you."

"Trust your instincts, Stormy," I said. "This visitor is no threat. Maybe he cannot hear me."

"My name is Geezer and I mean you no harm. I am homeless and

11

just looking for a safe place to spend the night," Geezer said. "May I come closer to you? I am very old and sometimes my ears do not work too well."

I heard Geezer come closer to the fence, separating the yard from the big house and driveway. I heard Stormy gasp as she told me that Geezer was a very big dog. This dog was a much bigger dog than either her Uncles Nitro or Lakota, who are both very big dogs.

Then to my surprise, I heard Stormy ask, "Would you like some dog biscuits, Mister Geezer?"

"That would be very nice of you, Young Lady Dog, if it is no trouble," Geezer said.

"I will be right back," Stormy said as I heard her scamper off to her doghouse for the biscuits.

I asked Geezer if he had been traveling long. He told me that when he became old, he lost his job as a guard dog. His employer left him on a road very, very far from what used to be his home. He could not find his way back. Once he realized he was lost, he stopped and asked himself why he should try to find his way back to a place where he was unwanted. He told me he has been traveling ever since. It has been a very long journey, and he is very tired. He told me the hardest part was being alone and unwanted.

As he was finishing his story, Stormy returned with the biscuits for the old dog.

"Thank you, Young Lady Dog. These biscuits are very good," Geezer said as he ate the biscuits.

"You are very welcome, Mister Geezer," Stormy replied. "My name is Stormy and this is my Uncle Rivers. He is blind."

"Well, I am very glad to meet both of you. I hope I did not disturb your sleep by coming into your yard this late," Geezer said.

"There is a bucket of water over by the shed if you are thirsty, Mister Geezer, so please help yourself," Stormy said.

As the old dog walked over to the bucket of water, I softly said to Stormy, "Well you sure changed your tune, Stormy. What made you decide to be so nice to the old dog?"

"Well, Uncle Rivers, I trusted my instincts as you suggested, and they told me that Mister Geezer is a nice old dog who is in need of some kindness." Stormy continued, "It is getting light, Uncle Rivers. Mike and the other dogs will be getting up soon."

I heard Geezer's paw steps as he walked back to us after he finished

drinking from the water bucket. I also heard all the dogs charging towards the fence barking at the old dog.

"Stop!" I barked, as I turned toward them. "This dog is my friend."

"And he is my friend also," Stormy barked.

"I was just leaving," Geezer said. "I want no trouble."

"No, Mister Geezer, you stay," Stormy said as I told the dogs Geezer's story.

"He has no home. He needs a place to stay. We are Huskies and we take care of our own," I said.

"But Rivers," Brownie said. "He is not a Husky."

Stormy surprised us with, "Well, maybe not. But he is a dog and he needs our help." I bet Stormy's Mom, Christmas, must be very proud of her daughter right now.

I heard the door to the big house open and Mike asked, "What is going on out here? Team, what are you up to?"

We all started barking at once at Mike, but unfortunately, he does not understand bark.

"Quiet!" Mike said and we all stopped barking. Stormy told me Mike walked over to Geezer.

"Hi Buddy. My, you are one big dog," Mike said. Stormy told me that Geezer sat down and raised his front paw the way dogs do to shake paws with a human.

Mike shook Geezer's paw. As he did, Mike looked at Geezer's paw pads. "You must have walked a long way to get these worn and cracked pads," Mike said. I heard Mike run his hands through Geezer's fur. "You are kind of thin too. I bet you have not had a decent meal for awhile." Stormy told me that Mike knelt in front of the big dog and put his hands on both sides of his face. "There is a lot of gray in your face, old Fella, but your eyes are clear. I bet you were dumped off somewhere, far away from your home."

Before Mike could finish, I heard Caitlyn ask, "Mike, is everything okay?"

Stormy told me Mike stood up and walked toward Caitlyn. At the same time, Randy came out of the house and said, "Oh, wow! Look at the size of that dog!"

Stormy told me that Mike held Caitlyn by her hand and walked with her to Geezer. "Hi Fella," Caitlyn said as she petted Geezer. Stormy said that Geezer licked her hand.

"Mike, may I keep him?" Caitlyn asked. "He likes me and I

would have a dog to play with while you and the team are on the trail. Please?"

Randy added, "Caitlyn has a point there Mike. We take all of the dogs with us when we run the trails. This old guy would be just the ticket for Caitlyn. He is big and appears to be gentle. I bet he would make a great companion dog for Caitlyn."

Mike said, "Well, we always have room for one more. But I think this dog should make that decision."

Geezer asked me what was wrong with Caitlyn's eyes. I told him that she was blind like me. "So, she needs a dog to take care of her," he said, with a lot of excitement in his bark. "I want the job!"

Stormy told me that Caitlyn asked Geezer if he wanted to be her buddy. He licked her face, she giggled, and, well after that, where you found one, you generally found the other.

Crash Time

After chow one night, we were all relaxing in the yard. Sometimes, after chow, we would swap trail stories for the enjoyment of the younger dogs. Nitro was the best storyteller, and sometimes his scary stories would raise the young dogs' neck fur. Sometimes mine also.

We were a bit shocked when Tundra asked her mother, "Momma, would you tell us the story of when you and Uncle Lakota were lost after the accident?"

The dogs became silent. We never talk about the accident. The accident was a dark time in Christmas' life. The accident happened shortly after her pups were born.

One of Mike's friends needed a hand training his team and asked Mike if he would bring a couple of us dogs over to help. Mike decided to take Lakota, Christmas and me. Mike felt it would be good for Christmas to get out of the yard for a while. Christmas was still grieving for Aunt Sandy. Remember, Sandy died protecting Christmas and the pups from a rouge wolf that snuck into our yard when the team was on a training run.

"How did you find out about the accident, Tunny?" Nitro asked. Nitro was very protective of Christmas.

"Well, Uncle Nitro, I overheard Mike and Mary talking about it. I never knew of an accident and I was curious. Did I do something wrong by asking about it?" Tundra asked.

"No, Tunny, you did nothing wrong," her Mother, Christmas, said. "I was lost after the accident. I feared I would never see you, my babies, my uncles, or Mary and Mike ever again".

"Christmas," I said, "you do not have to talk about this if you do not want to."

"I know, Uncle Rivers," Christmas replied. "But maybe it is best if I do tell the story. That is, if it is okay with Uncle Lakota. He was involved in it also."

Lakota said, "Little One, do what makes you feel good."

"Okay," Christmas said. She paused before starting her story. "It all started one morning when I heard Uncle Rivers barking, 'Wake up sleepy head, time to rise and shine'."

"Come on Christmas, we need to get ready for running the trails," my Uncle Lakota added.

"Ah, do I have to get up? I am so nice and comfy in my doghouse," I said.

"Gee, these young dogs just want to loaf. You are a Husky, Christmas, born to run the trails. Let us go. We are wasting daylight," Lakota said.

"He is right, Christmas," Uncle Rivers added. "We need to get started. Mike is getting the dog truck now."

"The dog truck! I hate riding in the dog truck," Christmas said. "I get tummy aches when I ride in it."

"That is okay, Christmas," I replied. "We all get sick at first, but you will get used to it as you get older. Besides, we get to run on the trails and that is the important thing."

I saw the truck parked in the driveway. Mike came over to us and told Uncle Lakota to go to the truck. Uncle Lakota ran to the truck, sat down, and waited for Mike to help him into the truck. Next, Mike put a leash on Uncle Rivers, and led him to the truck. Mike helped Uncle Rivers into the dog truck.

"Okay, Christmas Girl, your turn," Mike said as he clipped the leash on me. I guess he noticed that I was nervous about going because he knelt down next to me. He started petting my head as he said, "It is okay my Christmas Girl. You will be fine. It is a short trip to the trail. We have to go Christmas Girl."

Since I knew Mike loved me, I started walking with him to the dog truck. He gently helped me into it, made sure I was comfortable, and gave me a great ear rub.

Soon we were moving down the road. Uncle Rivers said, "Traveling makes me sleepy, think I will take a nap." Within moments, I heard him snoring.

"Rivers has the right idea, Christmas," Uncle Lakota said. He snoozes while we travel, makes the time go faster, you might want to try that."

"I am too nervous to nap, Uncle Lakota. Do you know when we will get there?"

"We will get there soon, "Uncle Lakota replied.

However, I did take Lakota's advice and tried to nap. I guess I dozed off because a horrible screeching sound woke me up. Then a thunderous crash that tossed me upside down.

"Hey, Lakota, are you okay?" It was Uncle Rivers.

"What happened?" I asked. Uncle Lakota never answered.

"Lakota, are you okay?" Uncle Rivers asked again – no reply.

"Okay Team, easy, I am here." It was Mike, I saw him rip open the side of the dog box that trapped us. Once freed, I ran off.

"Christmas stop!" Mike commanded, but I was too scared to obey.

I did not know where I was running to; I just knew I had to get away from the dog truck.

I heard some noise and looked around to see Mike on a 4-wheeler, racing after me. He raced ahead of me, stopped, got off the 4 wheeler and knelt down on one knee waiting for me to run up to him.

He called out, "Come on Christmas Girl, it is okay." However, I just kept on running and paid no attention to him. I was so scared that I kept on running.

When I slowed down, I noticed it was very foggy and I could not see very far. I was still scared. I heard voices calling me, friendly voices, but I was scared and did not come to them. Did I cause the accident? How come Uncle Lakota never answered Uncle Rivers? I was scared, confused and then I realized, I was lost!

I stopped and listened. I did not hear the voices any longer. Instead, I heard the sounds of big cars and trucks. I could not see them. Will they hit me? How will I find my way home? What about my babies, will I ever see my babies again? Who will take care of them? I was very scared, alone, and sad.

As I walked along the trail I was on, I noticed the noises of the cars and trucks sounded softer on my right side. I figured I was walking away from them. I saw some trees on my left side and realized I was near a forest. Maybe I can wait here until Mike finds me, I thought.

I must have fallen asleep. I woke up to strange voices and heard the snap of a leash. I looked around hoping I would see Mike or Mary, but I did not, only strangers.

"She sure is a pretty dog, bet we can get a lot of money for her," one of the strangers said.

"Let's get her into the box and get out of here. Her owner may come back looking for her," the other stranger said.

I barked, growled, and did everything I could, but they shoved me

into this box. I was trapped! The strangers put the box into a truck and covered it with a tarp. They drove off.

We did not go too far. When the truck stopped, the strangers took the tarp off the box I was in and put the box on the ground. They opened the box and I tried to run off, but they held on to the leash and put me into a pen.

After I settled down, I looked around. This yard was very dirty. I noticed there were many other dogs in the yard. They were all in pens or cages, and looked as scared as I was.

Night came. Many of the other dogs were crying for their human companions. I felt like crying also. Will I ever see my babies, or Mary, Mike, or my uncles again? I was thinking about this when I heard a voice say very softy, "Christmas, Christmas." It was Uncle Lakota.

"Uncle Lakota, are you okay?" I asked excitedly.

"Yes," he whispered, "but enough about me. We better get you out of that pen and away from this yard."

I watched him walk around my pen. I noticed the other dogs were quietly watching him also. He told me my pen sat directly on the ground. There is no wood or metal flooring like a cage. However, it was too large for him to knock over and the latch was too big for him to break.

"Dig here," Uncle Lakota said as he started pawing at a spot on the ground near the pen's fence. "Start digging here, Christmas, on your side of the fence, while I dig on my side. We will dig a tunnel to get you out of there."

I know Uncle Lakota is very smart and he loves to dig. I have seen some of the holes he has dug. They were huge. He digs very fast. I did as Uncle Lakota told me to do. Soon, there was a tunnel dug under the pen's fence. It was big enough for me to crawl through and out of the pen. I did it, and I was free!

"What about us?" Some of the other dogs cried out.

Uncle Lakota said, "Find a soft spot in your pen by the fence and start digging. We will start digging from the other side. Keep quiet. Do you want those men to come out here and stop us?"

Uncle Lakota and I walked around. Uncle Lakota noticed that some of the pen doors had weak latches that he could easily break. As he did, more dogs became free and helped dig the other dogs out of their pens. Soon all of the dogs were free. "Where do we go, what do we do now?" Some asked.

Uncle Lakota answered, "Be quiet and listen up. Go through the woods to the hard trail (road). You will find a trail next to the road.

Go left on the trail and follow it to the lake. Stay there, someone will find you. The freed dogs scampered off, leaving us alone.

"What about us, Uncle Lakota?" I asked.

"We will return to the crash site and wait for Mike to find us." He assured me Mike would come back for us.

As we walked through the woods to the road, I heard Uncle Lakota chuckle. "What are you laughing about?" I asked.

"I was imagining the look on the faces of those dudes when they see all the dogs are gone," Lakota said.

"Thank you for saving me," I said. "How did you know where I was?"

"I was thrown from the truck during the accident and was dazed. I woke up in the woods after everyone was gone. I went back to the crash site and found your scent. I followed it and saw you sleeping in the woods, but the strangers got to you before I could. Once they boxed you up, I followed the truck to their yard. I stayed in the woods until dark and then came to get you."

When we reached the road, I noticed that there were many cars and trucks moving on it. I was getting scared again. "Do we really have to cross the road, Uncle Lakota?" I asked. "Could we just stay here?"

"No, Little One," Uncle Lakota replied using my old nickname. "We must go to the other side of the road. It is safer there. The crash site is on the other side of the road and that is where Mike will return to look for us. Besides, there are several kennels and homes on that side where we might scrounge some chow."

"How are we going to get across the road to the other side?" I asked.

"We wait," he said. "Once there is a space between the cars and trucks, we make a run for it. When I give you the bark, run to the other side, and wait for me. Do not hesitate or one may hit you. Run as fast as you can, understand?"

We waited for what seemed like forever then I heard Lakota bark, "Go Christmas." I hesitated but started running across the road. I made it to the other side of the road. It was scary and my heart was pounding. A car just missed me, blowing a horrible sounding horn as it rushed passed me.

I turned around and saw Lakota making his run. He did not hesitate, running across the road.

"I hate these hard trails called roads. They are just too busy. The trucks and cars have no respect for dogs or humans," Lakota said.

Me too, I thought. I hate them also and I hope I never have to deal with them again.

Soon we were back at the crash site. There was not much to see. The truck was gone. All we could find was some broken plastic and the remains of the dog box that was on the truck.

"Rivers was here," Lakota said as he sniffed the snow.

"Well, he was in the truck with us," I said.

"True, but I smelled his scent in other areas besides the truck. That means Mike came back to look for us."

"Why would Mike bring Uncle Rivers?" I asked.

"Because," Uncle Lakota replied, "Rivers can smell our scents better than Mike can. He will help Mike find us. However, it is dark and they will continue searching once it gets light. So we need to find a safe place to stay until morning."

"What about food or water?" I asked.

Uncle Lakota said, "There is a stream a short ways from here. We can get a drink after we break through the ice. It has not been that cold lately so the ice will not be very thick. We can get a drink and then head to that falling-down cabin over there," Uncle Lakota said pointing with his paw to the cabin. "We can camp out in it for the night. We will look for food in the morning." We started walking to the stream. After we drank some water, we headed to the cabin.

When we arrived at the cabin, Uncle Lakota said, "I will check it out and chase away any critters that may be in there."

"Critters?" I asked.

"Yep, there are wild animals out here so we have to be careful," Uncle Lakota said, as he cautiously walked into the cabin through the broken front door.

Lakota came out and said it was safe for us to go in. We did and we both rested in the far corner of the cabin. The last I heard was Lakota whisper, "Good night Little One, we will get home soon."

When Uncle Lakota and I woke up the next day, we headed back to the crash site to wait for Mike to find us.

"We are too late," Uncle Lakota said. "Mike and Rivers have already been here and are headed south."

"Why would they be going that way when we are not there?"

"Because Mike saw you run that way. He never saw me. Rivers will follow your scent. He will lose it where the men boxed you up and put you in their truck," Uncle Lakota answered.

"But will Uncle Rivers smell your scent, Uncle Lakota?" I asked.

"Hopefully, yes, but your scent is stronger."

As we headed back to the cabin, I heard, "Christmas, Christmas, come on baby." I barked, but so did many other dogs and Mike could not hear me. Uncle Lakota explained to me that there were many dog lots in this area. Dogs are always barking around here. With Mike's bad hearing, he probably could not tell my bark from another dog's bark.

Then before we got back to the cabin, I thought I saw Mary. I barked. I saw her turn and call out, but she did not see me. She was very far away.

"Well, it looks like we are going to be here another night," Uncle Lakota said. His words did not make me a happy Husky.

We left the cabin and spent the day looking for food. The stream that we drank from had a few dead salmon that died after they spawned. Uncle Lakota told me that the cold water kept them from rotting too fast. We ate some and then it started to snow.

As we walked back to the cabin, I noticed footprints in the snow. I sniffed them and it was Mike and paw prints that smelled like Uncle Rivers. I told Lakota and he said that was great. "That means he moved his search back to this area."

When we got back to the cabin, there was a bowl of food, our food and our biscuits, plus two pig ears waiting for us. However, there was no Mike, Mary, or Uncle Rivers.

I was getting excited. Uncle Lakota said, "Do you know what this means Christmas? They know we are here. We just have to wait for them to find us. Eat up girl; I know you do not like fish. So eat what you want, while I enjoy chewing on this pig ear. Okay?"

It became dark as we finished eating. Uncle Lakota was telling me stories of running the trails, when all of the sudden, we heard something. I looked towards the sound and saw a pinpoint of light.

"Christmas, Lakota, come here." We were not sure if it was Mike. The night can play tricks with sounds. I looked towards the voice. It had to be Mike. I got up and ran as fast as I could. Uncle Lakota barked, "No! Wait!" The voice stopped, but I knew Mike was there and I ran faster. There was something blocking the trail. Nothing was going to stop me from going home with my Mike. I was determined to jump over this thing. As I did, I felt a leash snap onto my collar and a voice say, "Gottcha, Christmas Girl." I fell to the ground as Mike put

this huge body hug on me. Yes, it was my Mike. I was going home to Momma Mary, my babies, Uncle Rivers, and the rest of my family.

"Okay girl, lead me to Lakota!" I turned around and led Mike back up the trail towards the cabin.

"Lakota, Lakota come on boy," Mike called out. However, Uncle Lakota did not come out of the cabin. Where is he, I thought? I want to go home. We got to the cabin and Lakota was in the corner waiting for us.

Mike put a big hug on Lakota and snapped a leash on him. "It is time to go home, Lakota." We headed back down the trail at top speed. Mike said he never ran as fast as he did with the two of us pulling him down the trail.

We got to Mike's truck and I stopped short. There was no way I was getting into that truck. Mike opened the back and Lakota jumped in. I noticed this was not the truck with the dog box on it. Uncle Lakota said, "Come on Christmas, you want to go home?"

Mike knelt next to me. He rubbed my ears and told me it was okay. He stood up, picked me up, and gently put me in the back of the truck with Uncle Lakota. Mike closed the big door on the back of the truck and got into the truck, through a smaller door on the side of the truck. Once in, I heard Mike start the motor. Before we left, Mike pulled out a small box called a cell phone, and spoke these words into it, "Mary, I got both of them. We are on our way home."

Sky broke the silence in the yard as Christmas finished her story. "Wow, I was scared just listening to the story. You must have been very scared."

"But Uncle Lakota was not scared, he…," Stormy said, but before she could bark another word, Lakota interrupted her. "Not so fast, Young Lady Dog. I was very scared, Stormy." Lakota added, "There is nothing wrong with being scared as long as you do not let the fear get the best of you."

"You were so brave, Uncle Lakota, Tunny said.

"I do not consider what I did a brave thing. Christmas is family and we take care of each other. I am older and have been on my own for a long time while your Momma Christmas has been living here for most of her life. We all enjoy a great life here with Mike and Mary," Lakota continued. "Being lost made me realize how great we have it here. It is too bad that we seldom realize what we have until it is gone."

"Story time is over. It is time for Young Lady Dogs to go to bed,"

Christmas said. "Off to your doghouses girls. I will stop by shortly to check on you."

I heard the girls scamper off to their doghouse, giggling as young sister dogs will do. I heard all of the other dogs in the yard gather around Christmas and Lakota very quietly. I was a bit puzzled until I realized that none of us had heard the entire story. Christmas and Lakota never said much about their adventure when they came home, and no one asked them about it. None of us realized, or maybe wanted to realize, that our beloved Christmas and my best friend Lakota could have been lost forever!

It is as Lakota said. You do not know what you have until it is gone. I guess we are all lucky; we got it back, to appreciate and cherish.

War Dog

So far, it had been a cold and snowless winter. With no snow, the trails were too rough to run our sled on. Mike has been using the four-wheeler to exercise the team. Not a lot of fun, and frankly, I was bored. That was until Sky told me Mike was putting up the Christmas decorations. She told me about the big Santa Claus on the roof, all of the great-looking lights, and decorations Mike sets out for the holidays.

Christmas time! Wow, that makes me feel much better. We will run to the orphanage to deliver Christmas presents to the children and, of course, there is always lots of Mary's great chow. Even without snow, Christmas is a great time for us here at the Howlin' Rivers Home.

I was daydreaming about Christmases past, and really enjoying those great memories when I heard Mike come out of the big house and walk to the kennel.

"Come on Rivers, we are going into town," Mike said as he clipped the leash onto my collar.

"You also, Sky," Mike said as he hooked a neckline onto Sky's collar. I heard Mike hook the other end of the neckline to my collar.

"Wow, Uncle Rivers," Sky beamed, "we are going to town."

"Sky," I said. "You sure are excited about going to town."

"You are so right, Uncle Rivers. I have never been to town before. I heard you talking about going to town and it sounds like a super adventure. That is why I am so excited. This will be an awesome trip," She answered.

I really cannot blame Sky for being excited about her first trip to town. I remember my first trip to town. It is always fun going to town. This time Sky is going to go with us. I bet she will tell me everything she sees, which will make my trip even more enjoyable.

I am not sure how far the town is from our home, it sure seemed like a long ride to get there. Excitement does that, you know. It makes it seem much longer to get somewhere than it actually is.

Soon, the truck stopped and I heard Mike get out from the front

of it. I heard Mike walk to the back of the truck, open the tailgate, and open our travel crates. Of course, Sky is giving me a very detailed report on everything that is happening. Did I tell you that Sky is the most talkative dog in the kennel?

There were very few people on the trail. Mike was walking nice and slow. Sky told me that Mike was looking in the store windows. So, that was why we stopped so often.

I was really enjoying this nice slow pace, especially with Sky's detailed description of what she saw. Suddenly, I heard something. Yes, there was a lot of barking and a dog howling in pain.

"Sky," I asked, did you hear something?"

"Yes, Uncle Rivers. I did. It sounds…"

I interrupted her saying, "Sky, look to your left and tell me what you see."

"Uncle Rivers, there are two dogs fighting with another dog who looks hurt. We have to help him," Sky said.

Before I could say anything, Sky took off with me in tow. I felt the leash pull free from Mike's hand. I bet he was not expecting us to run off. I heard him yell, but Sky was not stopping. I could have stopped her, but there is a dog in need of our help. As we raced towards the dogs, Sky started barking and so did I. I heard Mike running behind us. Yes, he knows what is going on. I heard his footsteps stop. Sky told me Mike picked up a big stick that was on the ground. I heard Mike start to yell as he ran after us, towards the dogfight. I knew he was not yelling at us.

I guess the sight of us running at these two dogs scared them. Sky told me they ran off. She told me the hurt dog was lying down. When we got closer, Sky told me the hurt dog only had three legs. His right rear leg was gone, she said.

As I sniffed around the dog, Sky told me the dog was not a husky. The hurt dog was thin, dirty and looked like he had been on his own for a long time. I heard Mike kneel down next to the dog.

"Easy Buddy," Mike said. "Nobody is going to hurt you now. Let me see what I can do to help you." Mike then turned to us and said, "Sit down." We sat near Mike, but kept a lookout for those dogs. I bet they were still in the alley, waiting for a chance to attack.

Sky told me Mike took a tube of medicine out of his pocket and squeezed the medicine into the dog's wounds. He then took a handkerchief out of another pocket and wrapped it around the stump of the missing leg. It had the worst wounds.

"Okay Buddy, I have done the best I can do here for you. We are going to take you to Doctor Jim."

Sky told me that Mike stood up, looked around, and walked over to a big metal box with cardboard boxes in it. He took one of the smaller cardboard boxes out of the big metal box. Mike then laid the small box flat on the ground, and cut off one of the sides with his knife. When Mike finished cutting the box, he walked back to us, and gently slid the flat piece of the box under the dog.

"Okay Buddy, my dogs will give you a ride, sled dog style, on that piece of cardboard I put underneath you. I do not want to chance hurting you by carrying you. I want Doctor Jim to take a close look at your wounds before I try to carry you."

Sky explained how Mike tied our leash to the makeshift sled and gently walked with us to the truck. I heard the hurt dog breathing but not moving. I really hoped he would be okay.

When we got to the truck, Sky told me Mike opened the tailgate. "Okay Rivers, jump up and go into your travel crate," Mike said to me as I heard him unsnap the neckline from my collar. He gently guided me as I jumped up. I found the travel crate and sat in it. I heard Mike give Sky the same command. I heard her jump up onto the truck, and into her travel crate. I heard Mike close the gates to our travel crates. Sky told me Mike gently put the hurt dog into the truck with us. She told me that Mike covered the dog with the blanket I knew he kept in the truck. I heard Mike close the tailgate. His footsteps faded as he walked to the front of the truck.

While we were traveling to Doctor Jim's clinic, the dog gently barked to us. "I want to thank you for saving me back there. I had not eaten in several days and was very hungry. I found a piece of some human food. I think humans call it a sandwich. I was trying to find a place where I could eat it, when those two dogs jumped me."

I told the dog we had heard the barking and Sky started to charge to his rescue. She moved very quickly, jerking the leash out of our human's hands. The hurt dog said our barking, plus the sight of our human yelling and running with a big stick, probably caused the dogs to run away and leave him alone.

"Will you dogs get in trouble for running away from your human?"

"Probably not," I said. "Mike, our human, knows that we disobey him only if we have a really good reason. And I am sure, that once

he saw that you were in trouble, he knew we had a very good reason for doing what we did."

The dog replied, "You were very brave to do what you did. Not too many creatures would put themselves at risk to help a stranger in need."

"No, it was a very stupid thing I did." Sky said. "A good lead dog never leads her team into trouble. I led my Uncle Rivers into trouble. Big trouble if those two dogs decided to fight instead of run. My Uncle Rivers is blind."

"You are blind?" the hurt dog asked.

"Yes, but I do not allow that to stop me from enjoying life and helping others when I can. I tend to manage," I said.

I turned to Sky and said, "Sky, you really should not be so hard on yourself for running off like that. I could have stopped you. I was your co-leader. I could have told you to stop. However, I did not. You saw this dog in trouble. You saw he needed our help. You were willing to get involved. While being impulsive may not be a good thing for a lead dog, helping is. It is a sign of a true champion. This dog needed us. You did a good thing, Sky. I have done the same thing, charging in without thinking, to help someone in need. Sky, when someone needs help, you help."

"Are you doing okay, Mister Dog?" Sky asked.

"Yes, Young Lady Dog, I will make it. By the way, what are your names?"

Sky proceeded to tell the dog that my name was Rivers and her name was Sky. She told him where we lived, all about her sisters, her Momma Christmas, her uncles and our humans. As I said, Sky is the barker of the kennel.

Then the hurt dog told us his name was Stryker. He was a war dog. Sky asked him how he lost his leg. Stryker told us he was in the war zone with his human when he sensed some kind of explosive device. He stopped his human from walking on it, but in the process, Stryker stepped on it, and the explosive device blew off his leg. He told us that his handler, the surgeons, and veterinaries did a good job of saving him. He learned to walk on three legs. He can run, but not too fast. The military discharged Stryker because he lost his leg. He said he misses the military. They actually gave him a medal for saving his human handler.

Stryker told us a family adopted him after he left the military. He thought he found his forever home, but when the children realized Stryker was different from other dogs, they left him alone. Stryker said he was sad and confused since the children never played with him. Sometimes, Stryker said, the humans seemed to be uncomfort-

able around him. Maybe they were afraid of him due to his military training. Who knows, he said, but if they had doubts, why did they "adopt" him? One day he made up his mind. If he was going to be alone, he was going to be alone on his own and find his forever home on the other side of the fence. What is the point of being around humans that do not want to be around you, he asked? Stryker believed he would find a family or home that would really want him.

Stryker left during springtime and had been on the road ever since, never finding what he was looking for. When the cold weather settled in, he started to realize he was in trouble. See, he is not a husky and has a very thin coat. Coming from the war zone, where it is very hot, he did not adapt well to the cold. Frankly, he said, he really did not have the strength to fight those two dogs.

The truck stopped and the tailgate opened. I heard Doctor Jim's voice. He told Mike he would help Mike carry Stryker into the clinic. Before they moved Stryker, Mike opened the gates on our travel crates. As Doctor Jim and Mike carried Stryker, Mike told us to follow. Sky guided me off the truck and walked with me into the clinic.

"I am glad you told Sky and Rivers to follow us, Mike, I want to check them and make sure they were not hurt in the fight," Doctor Jim said.

After we were all inside the clinic, Sky told me that Doctor Jim and Mike gently placed Stryker on top of a table. Doctor Jim said, "Mike, look, he is a war dog, he is still wearing his military collar. I wonder if he has a microchip." Doctor Jim continued, "I will check once we treat his wounds."

Sky said Doctor Jim gave Stryker a shot and I heard Stryker go to sleep.

"Mike, I gave the dog a sedative so that I can stitch up some of his open wounds. There is not a lot of bleeding and I do not think there are any broken bones. However, he is very weak and may not have the strength to recover. He is very thin and will need some time to get his strength back. Whoever amputated his leg did a good job. It appears the stump was the target of the dogfight. I am concerned about infection and damage to the remaining parts of his hip and the leg stump. There is a lot of scar tissue on his chest area. I bet he has one good story to tell, too bad he cannot tell it."

A few seconds of silence passed before Doctor Jim asked Mike. "Do you want to leave him here at the clinic?"

"I knew he was in bad shape when I worked on him after the dogfight. I noticed the collar. I recognized it. I noticed the scar tissue. That is shrapnel scarring. I bet he stepped on a landmine." Mike

paused and then said, "No, Doctor Jim, he goes home with us. We will make room for him. He deserves something much better than being homeless. If he is going to die, let him die at our place, among those who care about him," Mike said.

I only heard that tone in Mike's voice once before and that was when Sandy died. I guess that Stryker being a war dog must have significant meaning for Mike. I wonder if Mike had a war dog when he was in the Air Force.

After Doctor Jim checked us out, Mike took us back to the truck. Sky told me that Doctor Jim and Mike carried Stryker and gently placed him on the blanket that Mike used to cover him when we left town. Stryker was still asleep.

Doctor Jim reminded Mike about Stryker's medicine. Doctor Jim wanted Mike to call him if Stryker did not improve. He told Mike that the next day or so would be critical. If Stryker makes it though the night, he has a good chance of recovery. Hmm, Doctor Jim did not seem too optimistic. Things do not sound too good for Stryker.

Once we got back to our home, Mike put us in the kennel and Sky told me that Mike carried Stryker into the warming hut. The other dogs in the kennel asked us about the hurt dog.

Before I could bark a word, Sky was telling them the entire story, including Stryker's past. She told them that he was hurt very badly and Doctor Jim was not too sure if Stryker would recover.

The dogs were excited to have a guest at our kennel, but sad that Stryker was in such bad shape. Nitro was upset. "He saved his human and then he is abandoned, left to fend for himself. I would like to meet those dogs that attacked him. I would give them a shakin' they would never forget. No respect for those who have given so much." As you know, Nitro is the biggest dog on our team.

Christmas interrupted him. "Uncle Nitro, if you were there, those bad dogs would never have dared to attack Mister Stryker. Unfortunately, you were not there. Sky and Rivers were. Uncle Rivers, you know that fighting is not good. It was a good thing that Mike was there." Christmas continued, "And for you, Young Lady Dog Sky, while I admire your courage and willingness to help a dog in need, we really need to talk about acting recklessly."

I sensed that Momma Christmas was in her scolding mode. "Christmas," I said. "Do not be too hard on Sky. She knew she was wrong for leading me into what could have been a bad situation, and I have already spoken to her about it," I continued. "Now Little One (I used her old nickname

29

deliberately), before you go too far, you do remember when you were ready to tangle with a wolf that wanted to hurt one of your friends? I guess Sky was just following in your paw steps, Momma Christmas."

A moment passed, as I knew Christmas was remembering when a wolf threatened her friend Sunny.

"You know, Uncle Rivers, you are right. I guess I cannot blame Sky for doing something I did myself," Christmas replied.

Smart lady dog I thought.

I heard Brownie say, "You mean we have a real war hero here with us, Doc?"

Doc replied, "It seems so. Stryker was a war dog and war dogs protect their humans. Apparently, Stryker did his job. Too bad he suffered so much afterwards."

"Yes, it is so sad that Stryker gave so much and received so little in return," Ugly replied. Yes, there is a serious side to Ugly.

"Momma Christmas," it was Stormy. "You think that Mike will let Mister Stryker stay here with us? We got plenty of room and I would share my dog biscuits with him."

"Me also," Tunny chimed in. "And my tennis balls. I wonder if he has ever chased one. If he does not know how, I could teach him."

"That is not for me to decide. That is Mike's decision to make," Christmas answered. "But first, Mister Stryker needs to get well. And from hearing what Sky and Uncle Rivers said, he may not."

I was amazed. The outpouring of feelings for Stryker, a virtual stranger, was very touching. Nitro's response was typical Nitro; he would protect those who cannot protect themselves. The respect and concern the dogs displayed for Stryker's sacrifices amazed me. I was becoming angry and walked away from the group of dogs in the kennel. I wanted to be alone for a little while as I thought about this war dog. Stryker had been searching for his forever home. He may have found it, but may not live long enough to enjoy it. That bothered me.

I was deep in my thoughts when I heard a voice ask, "Rivers, are you angry?" It only took me a second to recognize her bark. It was Sandy. You may remember that Sandy was Mike's housedog. She died protecting Christmas and her puppies from a rogue wolf. Sandy has become our Guardian Angel Dog and watches over all of the dogs in our kennel.

"Sandy, you know my feelings?" I asked.

"I know you, Rivers. You have an extreme sense of fairness and what has happened to Stryker does not seem fair to you." Sandy said.

"Rivers, nothing in this world is fair. Life gives you a trail to race. The way you run it determines how you finish your race. Like you, Stryker's race has been pretty rough at times."

I asked, "Is he going to make it? I bet Mike would let him stay here and have his forever home with us. You could..."

Sandy cut me short. "I cannot answer your question or know what Mike may do. I have no power to influence his decision," Sandy said. "The will to survive comes from within you, Rivers. So, if Stryker is going to make it, it will be totally up to him." Sandy continued, "As for Mike's decision, you know Mike as well as I do, he is a human, and humans are unpredictable."

"You know, Rivers," Sandy continued, "I heard from Christmas and her babies about Stryker already, and also from several of your teammates. Their outpouring of concern shows the true champions they all are. I am very proud of all of them, especially Christmas and her babies. She has done a great job raising them."

I could hear the pride in Sandy words. "Well Sandy, you were a pretty good role model," I said.

She nudged me and was gone.

Mike interrupted my thoughts when he started to bang the ladle on the food bucket. That is Mike's way of telling us it is chow time. It was Christmas Eve and the food was special. While I ate, my thoughts returned to Stryker. Sky told me he was still asleep from the shot Doctor Jim gave him. I bet Sky has been watching over him. I am sure Mike will have a bowl ready for Stryker when, and if, he wakes up.

After chow, we all milled around the kennel barking about the events of the day and getting excited about what happens on Christmas Day. Right after morning chow, Mike puts on his red Santa suit, and loads the sled with gifts and goodies for the children at the orphanage. Then after putting us into our team positions, we race down the trail to the orphanage. Mike will give out the gifts. After that, he will take us off the gang line and let us play with the children. Even Nitro, as big and gruff as he is, loves playing with the children. Actually, we all like to play with our friends at the orphanage. Later that day, we will race home to more of Mary's great chow. After chow, Mike will give each of us a present. I wonder what he has for us this year. If I had a choice, it would be that Stryker became well and lived with us. That would be one great present, not only for me, but more so for Stryker. I bet the other dogs feel the same way as I do. We have so much and Stryker has nothing and no one.

Later, when Mike came out of the big house to give us our bedtime treats and ear rubs, he said that Sky and I would sleep in the warming hut with Stryker. We waited patiently as Mike gave each of the dogs a biscuit and made a big fuss over them before they went to their doghouses.

"Come with me," Mike said to us. We followed him into the warming hut. Sky told me that Mike moved Stryker into a stall so that he could rest on a big pile of straw. Stryker was still asleep. His breathing was deep and even, which was a good sign. Sky told me that Mike applied some more medicine to his wounds, and gave Stryker another shot, just as Doctor Jim did.

"Sky and Rivers, you will sleep in here with our guest. When he wakes up, bark and howl for me." Sky told me that Mike covered Stryker with a blanket, gave him an ear rub, and left the hut.

After a while, I said to Sky, "I have to go to the bathroom, I will be back very soon."

"Okay Uncle Rivers, I will sit right here by Mister Stryker until you get back. Then I have to go too. Okay?"

"Sure," I said as I left the hut.

I have a spot in a corner of the yard where I go to do my thinking. I went there after going to the bathroom. I silently howled my prayers for Stryker to get well and for Mike to let him stay with us. I know this is the "Season of Giving". I hope that the magic of the season will allow Stryker to recover and find his forever home with us. As I walked back to the warming hut, I felt snow falling gently on my face. Yes, I thought, how nice, snow for Christmas!

When I returned, Sky left to do her business. Stryker was still resting peacefully.

"Uncle Rivers," Sky whispered to me, "I saw Aunt Sandy when I was outside. She was checking on Momma Christmas and my sisters, Tundra and Stormy. When she saw me, she stopped and told me how very proud she was of me. There were tears in her eyes."

I replied, "I think your Aunt Sandy checks on you, your Mom, and your sisters very often, Sky. You all were, and continue to be, very special to her. You were the babies she never had. Aunt Sandy feels the same way about your Momma Christmas." Silently, I wondered if Sandy visits Mike also. I continued, "I think we need to get some sleep, Sky. It has been a very exciting day and we will have a big day tomorrow at the orphanage."

"Yes, Uncle Rivers, you are right. I am getting sleepy," Sky said and soon I heard her start to snore.

I guess I went to sleep also, but woke very fast when I heard, "Excuse me Rivers, where is the bathroom?"

Before I could say anything, Sky said, "Mister Stryker, you are standing up! Are you okay?"

"Yes, I think so, but I really need to go to the bathroom," he said.

We walked out of the warming hut and both Sky and I started to bark and howl. Soon the other dogs were up and standing around us. Soon, Mike joined us.

After Stryker went to the bathroom, Sky introduced him to all of the other dogs in the yard. Stormy told me Mike knelt down next to Stryker and checked his wounds.

"You are looking real good," Mike said. I heard the smile in his voice. "Yes, looking real good. But it is too cold for you out here, so how about if we all go back into the warming hut."

We all followed Mike into the warming hut. Mike told us he was getting morning chow and left the hut. Soon, all of the dogs left the hut. I stayed behind with Stryker.

Stryker asked, "What is going on?"

"You got me on that one," I answered. "However, I do know those dogs did a lot of wishing and praying for your recovery last night."

"Well, I really do appreciate that, but I need to go," Stryker said. "I am on a mission to find my forever home, a place where I belong and will be loved. Some place where I will be safe and have a human companion." Stryker paused, then said, "Your place is nice, very nice, but...."

I heard all of the dogs return. When Stormy came by my side, she told me that the dogs brought gifts for Mister Stryker.

Stormy told me that Stryker sat down as each of the dogs gave him their presents. Nitro was first and gave Stryker a rawhide chew. Then Ugly gave him a biscuit and made him laugh with his Ugly Jig. Each dog gave something to Stryker.

Stryker asked, "What is the meaning of this?"

Stormy told me that her Momma Christmas sat down in front of Stryker. Christmas said, "Our human, Mike, named me Christmas because I was found on Christmas Eve by my Uncles Rivers, Nitro, Doc, Lakota, Brownie, and Ugly. What my uncles and my babies are doing is wishing you a Merry Christmas. We discussed it and we all want you to stay here with us. We want you to make this your forever home."

Before anyone could bark anything, I heard Mike walk into the hut with the food bucket.

"Hmm, it seems we have a party going here," Mike said. "What is the occasion? Let me think. Yes," Mike said as he chuckled. "It is Christmas Day and Christmas is the time for giving. So," Mike paused, "how about we give this war dog his forever home, he can stay for good. And, I bet he could use a nice warm dog coat and a brand new collar."

Lakota told me that Mike slipped the new collar on Stryker after removing his old one. The new one was green and gold, our team colors! Then Mike put the dog coat on him. Lakota said that the coat had the hole covered where the missing leg would be, and there was a pocket for the stump to go in. Lakota said that the pocket would keep the stump warm, while both protecting and supporting it.

Lakota told me that Mike, knelt down next to Stryker, and said, "Well, Buddy, do you want to stay with us? Do you want to join our team?"

Lakota told me that Mike held out his right hand. While I could not see them, I knew all of my teammates were watching this war dog very carefully, wondering what he would do. Stormy told me that Stryker looked at each one of us dogs. Then, after what seemed like forever, Stryker put his paw into Mike's hand and barked, "Yes!"

Ironically, Mike decided to name Stryker, Stryker, in honor of some of Mike's friends serving with an Army Stryker unit in the war zone.

Christmas and the Moose

$\mathbf{M}$ike surprised us with a short springtime trail run. The mud, caused by the melting snow, finally dried on the trails, and the temperature, while not warm, was very pleasant. Mike decided to take just the girls, Lakota and I. He told us this would be a short three-mile run or so with a nice long break by the lake. Mike joked that he may even give us a bath in the lake. Fat chance, I thought. Knowing Lakota and how much fur he has, Mike would be the one dripping wet from a doggie water whip when Lakota shook all the water off himself. Bottom line is this. If Mike wants to bathe us, he has to catch us.

Mike had Christmas and Sky in lead position with Stormy and her twin, Tundra, in the swing dog position. Lakota and I were in the wheel position, just ahead of the training cart Mike used for this run. I am sure on the return run he will let Stormy and Tundra run in the lead positions. Who knows, maybe I will get a chance to lead also! The run to the lake is a short one on nice flat trails. A good run if you have not run for a while.

The first run of spring is always a nice, fun, run. The pace is gentle since we need to get back into shape after waiting for the trails to dry out. At the pace we were going, I could get a good whiff of all the nice spring smells of flowers, young sweet grass, and moose.

Moose, I thought. Yes, there would be moose in this area. The lake is a nice area for moose. Momma moose have their babies near the lake in the springtime. Bears are not too common in this area, but wolves are, and like bears, are natural predators of moose.

Another nice thing about running to the lake is that when we get there, Mike lets us off the gang line and we can wander a bit. Soon Mike gave us the "Whoa" command, his command for us to stop. After we stopped, Mike let us off the gang line so we could roam by the lake. Lakota and I headed to the lake for a drink of the icy cold lake water. Yes, it was nice and refreshing. Lakota told me that the girls were playing in the soft grass, while Christmas was sitting next to Mike.

When we finished drinking and were walking back to where Mike was sitting, Lakota told me he wanted to take a nap by Mike. He asked Christmas if she wanted to take a walk with me.

"Sure Uncle Lakota, I will take a walk with Uncle Rivers," Christmas replied as I heard her get up and walk over to me.

I heard Christmas tell her girls, "Uncle Rivers and I are going for a short walk up the trail. I want you young lady dogs to stay close to the lake where Mike can keep an eye on you."

"Yes, Momma," was the reply from her pups.

We did not get too far when I heard a crying sound. "Christmas, I hear something crying to your left. Do you see anything?" I asked.

"I see some trees but nothing else, Uncle Rivers." Then she asked,"Do you want to walk over there and check it out?"

"Yes," I said as we started to head that way. The crying sound was getting louder and I heard something else, wolves, or wild dogs.

Christmas, there are wolves or wild dogs among those trees we are heading to. We need to be..."

"Uncle Rivers, there is a very small baby moose and the wild dogs are chewing on a carcass of...," Christmas interrupted.

"The mother moose, I bet," I said to Christmas.

"Uncle Rivers, we have to save that baby moose from those wild dogs."

Before I could answer Christmas, we both heard, "Stop that crying, Brat. We will eat you next." We heard a dog bark.

I heard Christmas let out one mean, loud growl as she raced to where the baby moose was. I ran with her and heard her bark, "You are not going to touch that baby."

I caught up to Christmas and stood her. I know we were between the wild dogs and the baby moose. I was not sure how many wild dogs there were, maybe 4 but that was just a guess.

"Go home, pretty lady dog and take your buddy with the funny-looking eyes with you. That baby moose is our dessert," one of the wild dogs replied.

Before Christmas or I could answer, I heard Stormy growl, "We are not going anywhere. We are staying right here and protecting that baby from you." I heard two more sets of paw steps and knew that Tundra and Sky were with Stormy, standing with us between the baby moose and the wild dogs.

"Oh golly gee, we are so scared of you pretty dogs," another of the wild dogs said mocking us. "Go back home to the laps you came from."

"You dogs really are not getting the point here, are you?" It was Lakota. "You are not going anywhere near that baby moose."

Now Lakota is a very big and powerful dog. He is very protective of Christmas, her babies and me. He can be a very intimidating when he needs to be. I know he will not back down. This was becoming a very dangerous situation. We cannot abandon the baby moose.

"Team, down!" was the command followed by "Bam, Bam, Bam, Bam, Bam." Then, a very eerie softness filled the air. I knew Mike had no choice but to shoot them to protect us. Lakota told me that there were five wild dogs.

"Anyone hurt?" Mike asked as I heard him move among us. We were all still down on the ground as he commanded.

"That was one foolish idea you had for a turf fight with those wild dogs," Mike started to scold us. "I thought I taught... What is that sound?"

Lakota told me that Christmas got up and walked over to where the baby moose was laying down. I heard the baby crying.

"Christmas," Mike softly asked. "What do you have there?" I heard Mike walk towards the crying sound.

"A baby moose! From the looks of it, it is only a few hours old. I bet the mom gave birth to the baby just before those wild dogs came on the scene and attacked her," Mike said. Lakota told me that Christmas was sitting near the baby, comforting it.

"So, this is why you were going to fight the wild dogs. You were protecting this baby moose," Mike said.

I knew Mike would not be angry with us for what we did. He knows we protect each other and, at times, protected others who were in trouble. Therefore, I was a bit surprised when he started to walk away from the baby moose. "Okay, team, back to the training cart."

He was leaving the baby moose and wanted us to follow him. This is totally out of character for Mike. He would never leave someone or something who needed his help. Lakota told me that Christmas and her girls sat by the baby moose. We sat also.

Lakota told me that Mike stopped walking away when he realized we were not following him.

"We cannot take this moose with us, Team, it is against the law. Besides, I do not know how to take care of a baby moose," Mike said.

Christmas can be very stubborn. She is also very smart and knows that Mike will not leave us here. She is also a momma dog and I bet

37

her motherly instincts have kicked in to care for this baby moose. From what Lakota described to me, it looks like all of the lady dogs are mothering this baby moose.

Mike said, "Okay Christmas, I get the picture, but let me warn you, once we get this moose out of here and back home, it needs to go to the zoo or the animal conservatory. So do not start thinking you have another baby to care for. You understand, Christmas?"

Christmas barked once telling Mike she understood. Mike can be stubborn also, but I think he knew that this baby would not survive alone in the woods without a mother or kin moose to care for it.

I heard the baby moose whisper to Christmas, "Miss Christmas, what is going to happen to me? Where are we going? What is that creature that was talking to you?"

Christmas replied, "We are taking you to our home to take care of you for awhile. You will be safe with us. That creature is a human and his name is Mike. He takes care of us. We are his family."

The baby moose asked, "Will he take my momma, I know she is hurt."

Christmas gently said, "I am sorry, but your momma died protecting you from the wild dogs."

I heard the baby moose start to cry again. "I have no momma?"

Lakota told me that all the lady dogs cuddled with the baby moose to comfort her.

The baby moose asked Christmas, "Will you be my momma?"

Christmas gently said, "I am a dog and you are a moose. I can be your friend, but not your momma."

"Moose, dog, what are those?" Asked the baby moose, "who will teach me?"

"We will talk later," Christmas said, "right now we need to get you up and start walking so we can take you home."

Lakota told me that the baby moose stood up, a bit shaky at first, but Christmas and her pups gave the baby moose lots of encouragement. Soon, the baby moose was walking with Christmas. We all started to walk towards Mike.

I heard a soft chuckle and knew it was Mike. I could picture this parade in my mind, Mike in lead, followed by Christmas and the baby moose with Stormy, Tundra and Sky following them and of course, Lakota and me bringing up the rear.

When we reached the training cart, Christmas told the baby moose that she had to let Mike pick her up and put her in the cart's basket. After that, we would give her a great ride to our home. Lakota told me that the baby moose sat down after Mike gently picked her up and put her in the cart's basket. The baby moose said that Mike's fur (beard) tickled her nose. Stormy told me that the baby moose calmly watched as Mike put us back into our team positions. Only this time, Christmas was in the wheel with me. Lakota moved to the lead position with Stormy. Tundra and Sky were the swing dogs.

Before we left, Christmas told me that Mike removed the cell phone from his pocket and started to talk into it.

"Hi Mary, this is Mike. No, I am okay, but we do have a guest I am bringing home. You will not believe what happened at the lake. I will tell you when I get home. Would you run over to Farmer Matt's place and borrow one of the baby bottles he uses to feed the baby calves? You might want to get about 5 gallons of milk from him also. Would you ask Randy and Caitlyn to research the internet for feeding instructions for baby moose? Gotta go." I bet Mary was surprised.

We took off for home after Mike finished talking to Mary. Christmas told me that Mike put the cell phone back into his pocket. I heard Christmas softly talking to the baby moose, who sounded as if she was really enjoying her first dogsled ride. I wonder how many moose have ever traveled by dogsled.

I bet you can picture the excitement at our home when the Team stopped in the yard and Mike helped Mindy out of the cart's basket. Oh, yes, we named her on the trail as we headed home. Mindy said she really liked her new name.

I heard Mary, Randy, and Caitlyn come out of the house.

"Mike, how come you are holding a baby moose in your arms?" Randy asked.

Before Mike could answer, Mary said, "You are not keeping a moose here, Mike. Are you?"

"A baby moose!" Caitlyn exclaimed. "Please let me pet it?" She asked. Stormy told me that Randy helped Caitlyn so she could touch the baby moose in Mike's arms. Stormy told me that the moose seemed to enjoy the attention and affection.

While this was going on, Lakota told the rest of the team what had happen at the lake. Amazingly, my teammates accepted that this moose needed our help, even though all of us, except the lady dogs, have encountered moose on the trail. We all felt that Mindy should

stay here for a while. Deep inside, I knew that the longer Mindy stayed with us, the harder it would be for the lady dogs, especially Christmas, to let her go.

"Randy," Mike said, "please find the biggest collar in the warming hut for our guest here. After that, get one of the stalls ready for her."

As Randy ran off to get the collar, I heard Mary say, "Mike, you cannot be serious about keeping this moose." Stormy told me that Mary moved closer to Mike just so she could give Mindy a few ear rubs.

"No," Mike said. "I really had no choice but to bring her home." Mike then told the story of what happened at the lake. Apparently, Lakota never did nap. When Mike saw Stormy, Sky, Tundra, and Lakota race towards the woods, he chased after them. He told Mary he had no choice but to shoot the wild dogs. When our dogs would not leave the baby moose, Mike realized he could not leave the little orphan alone in the woods. He knows that this moose can never return to the wild. The more it interacts with humans and domesticated dogs, the more dependent it becomes on humans for survival.

Stormy told me that Randy returned with a collar and leash. Mike put Mindy down. He then put the collar on the moose and snapped the leash. Mike then said, "Randy, please take the team off the gang line and remove their harnesses. Then bring Christmas to the warming hut and join us there, I bet this baby moose is hungry."

After a short time, Randy came out to where the team was. He gave us fresh water and some treats. Lakota told me that Randy closed the warming hut when he came into the yard. I bet they are feeding Mindy and do not want her disturbed while she eats.

Mike found a home for Mindy at the Animal Conservatory, a super nice place for orphaned wild animals. While I know it was hard for Christmas and her girls to see Mindy go, they knew it was for the best. There were other baby moose and some momma moose at the conservatory. We visit the conservatory often since it is not far from where we live. Mindy tells us she is having a great time at the conservatory. She really loves it there. I bet that makes Christmas and her pups feel better and proud that they helped Mindy when she could not help herself. During one of our visits, Sky made the remark that she was amazed at how big Mindy was becoming. Well, Sky, I thought, Mindy is a moose, and moose get very, very big.

Fur Creatures One and All

You know, time flies when you are having fun, and before I knew it, it was Christmas time again at the Howlin' Rivers Home. You could feel the excitement in the air. Mary and Caitlyn were busy baking goodies and wrapping presents for our friends at the orphanage. Mike and Randy were doing some training runs with us. They also were busy running errands, and finishing chores to get ready for the holiday season. So far, it has been a poor snow season so the training runs have been few and far between.

However, that changed after the big storm hit and dumped plenty of snow on us. After the storm stopped, we all rushed out of our doghouses into the yard, and played in the snow like little puppies. It sure was fun. In all of the excitement, I noticed that I did not hear Tundra. Normally, Tundra is the most fun loving dog in our yard. She is always playing and running around, especially if there are tennis balls to chase. Therefore, it was unusual not to hear Tundra in the yard, yelping with glee as she romped in the snow.

I wandered by her doghouse and said, "Tundra, come on out of your doghouse. The snow is great to play in."

"No thanks, Uncle Rivers, I think I will just lay in my doghouse for a while."

Now that was strange. Tundra never stays in her doghouse when it is fun time in our kennel.

"You okay, Tunny?" I asked.

"Yes, Uncle Rivers, I just do not feel like playing now."

"Okay," I said. I started to walk off, but turned my head back to the direction of her doghouse when I heard, "It is okay, Mister Bunny. Please try to eat something while I keep you warm. You are still shivering."

I heard a very faint, little voice cry, "I am so tired and cold. I do not feel very well, Miss Tundra."

"Tundra," I said gently, "Do you have a something in your doghouse?"

I heard movement in her doghouse and felt her face very close to

mine. Whispering, she said, "Yes, Uncle Rivers, I have a very small bunny in here. I found him in the far corner of the yard a few nights ago. He was very weak. He asked me for help. I could not refuse him. I have been giving him some of my food and trying to keep him warm."

How come you did not tell us?" I asked.

Tundra replied, "I do not know, Uncle Rivers. Maybe I was afraid my sisters would make fun of me, or my other uncles might think I was a weak dog because I was trying to help this little bunny. Maybe I was afraid they would chase it out of the yard. Maybe I was afraid that my momma would tell me to let it go. I could not do that. I felt I had to help Mister Bunny." Tundra was very upset. "But, I am afraid, Uncle Rivers. Mister Bunny is very sick and I cannot help him. I do not know what to do."

Yes, dogs do cry and Tundra was on the verge of crying. She is a very young dog herself. "Tundra, you did a good thing by trying to help Mister Bunny," I said. "Let me get a bit closer so I may hear him breath and touch him with my nose."

"Okay Uncle Rivers, but please be gentle, Mister Bunny hurts when he moves."

"Hello Mister Bunny, my name is Rivers," I said. "I just want to check on you. I am not going to hurt you."

I touched the bunny's ear with my nose. The bunny felt warm to me and his breathing was very shallow. This bunny was in serious trouble.

"Mister Rivers," the bunny whispered, "I am very old, and I am going to die. I do not think Miss Tundra realizes that. She was very kind and took me in so that I would not be alone. All of my family and friends live very far away. I was trying to get to them, but I became too tired and weak. Miss Tundra found me several days ago foraging for food near your yard. I must have fainted because the next thing I knew, I was in her doghouse, under some warm straw."

I do not think Tundra heard what the bunny said. I moved my head out of the opening of the doghouse and said, "Tundra, we need to get Mike out here to help us. Mister Bunny is very sick and there is nothing that we dogs can do for him."

Tunny asked, "How do we get Mike out here?"

"Start barking," I told her. As we did, all of the other dogs in the yard came by. I told them what was going on while Tundra barked. I never heard Tunny bark that way before. Tunny barked as if she was

crying out for help. I am sure that if none of us started to bark, Tunny's barking would have gotten Mike's attention.

Before long, I heard Mike come racing into the yard. "Tunny, what is the matter girl? You okay?" Mike asked.

Tunny was out of her doghouse by now and Stormy told me that Tundra was barking directly at the opening of her doghouse. She was telling Mike that the problem was in her doghouse.

"Is there something in your doghouse, Tundra?" Mike asked as I heard him kneel down to look into her house.

"Tunny!" Mike said. "Where did this bunny come from?" After a short pause, Mike said, "This bunny is very sick, Tunny. We need to get it to Doctor Jim immediately." As Mike raced out of the kennel to the truck, he said to Mary, who Lakota told me was on the porch, "Call Doctor Jim and tell him we are bringing a sick bunny to his clinic. I am also taking Tundra and Rivers since they were near the bunny and they may have caught whatever made this bunny sick."

I heard the truck door open and Mike told Tundra to jump onto the front seat. Next, he grabbed my collar and told me to jump as he gently pulled up on my collar to guide me up, onto the front seat. I heard him slide in next to me. Tundra told me Mister Bunny was in Mike's lap. Mike told both of us to sit still.

Doctor Jim's clinic is not far away from our home and we got there in no time at all. "Hi Mike, Rivers and Tundra, let me take a look at your bunny," Doctor Jim welcomed us. Mike grabbed my collar to lead me out of the truck as he told Tundra to come with us.

While I cannot see the room we were in, I know I have been there before. This is where Doctor Jim made me pain free.

Tundra told me that Doctor Jim gently examined Mister Bunny. I heard Doctor Jim say, "Mike, this bunny is not sick; he is dying of old age. I think he may also have some internal injuries, but I cannot be sure. I can gave him an injection to make him pain free, but I do not expect him to last much more than few hours. I can put him to sleep if you want." Doctor Jim continued, "It was a good idea to bring Tundra and Rivers in for a check. Dogs can catch things from wild animals."

"Just make him pain free, Doctor Jim," Mike said. "As long as the bunny is not suffering, we will take him back to our yard so he will not die alone. I am not sure what is going on here, but I found him in Tundra's doghouse and it looked like she had been trying to care for

him. I found bits of her food in there and bunched-up straw in her house. It looked like a small nest. I think Rivers figured out what was going on and had Tundra bark, so I would come to the kennel."

"Smart dogs you have there, Mike. I would never imagine a dog trying to care for an old bunny," Doctor Jim said. "Well this is Christmas and the time for wondrous things. It is too bad that many humans do not act like your dogs. If they did then, this world would be a much better place to live in."

"Yep, you are right there, Doctor Jim," Mike said. "All we can do is work to make this world better for those around us." Mike continued, "We need to get back to the homestead, Doctor Jim. Since tomorrow is Christmas, we need to get ready for the orphanage run and... well..." Mike's voice trailed off, as if he was holding back his words for Tunny's sake. She is a very loving and sensitive dog. I know she is going to be very upset when and if Mister Bunny dies tonight.

I leaned up against Tundra. She was trembling as she pleaded, "Oh, please do not die, Mister Bunny." She cried as we walked back to the truck.

"Merry Christmas Mike, Tundra, and Rivers," Doctor Jim said as we left. We stopped and I heard Mike turn around and say, "Merry Christmas to you also, Doctor Jim. "And thank you."

"Tundra," Doctor Jim called out as I heard him walk to Tundra. "What you tried to do for that bunny was terrific. Your act of kindness is what this season is really all about. Thank you. Tundra, you are like your buddy, Rivers, a very special dog. Take care."

I hoped Tunny understood what Doctor Jim was saying. Doctor Jim has known Tunny since she was born and has been her vet ever since. Doctor Jim treats all of us like we were his own dogs.

Back at the yard, Mike took us into the warming hut. Tundra told me that Mike placed Mister Bunny on a big pile of straw. Then, Mike told Tunny that she could lie down next to Mister Bunny if she wanted to. I heard Tundra softly crawl onto the straw next to Mister Bunny.

I heard the other dogs come into the warming hut, as Mister Bunny started to talk to Tundra. Mister Bunny's voice was very weak. "Miss Tundra, I know I am dying, I knew that when you found me the other day. Thank you for caring for me, keeping me warm, and sharing your food with me. You did not have to do that since I am a stranger to you, and especially since I am not a dog," Mister Bunny continued. "I am a very old bunny, Miss Tundra, and all of my family and friends are either gone or moved very far away. I was alone when you found me. Your caring for me kept me from being both lonely and alone during this beautiful season of Christmas. Please do not be sad, Miss Tundra, you did a very beautiful thing. Not too many creatures would take an old bunny into their home, or even share a meal with him. You made my last Christmas a very beautiful thing, Miss Tundra. Thank you."

I heard a soft gasp and knew Mister Bunny was gone. Christmas told me that Tunny gently poked the bunny with her nose. "Mister Bunny," she said softly, "Mister Bunny." Then she started to howl the most sorrowful howl I have ever heard. We all joined Tunny, howling our prayers into the night for Mister Bunny.

After they finished howling, the other dogs left the warming hut. I stayed with Tundra. Mike told Tundra that he had a small box for Mister Bunny and would bury him in our special garden where Mike buried Sandy, Mike's beloved housedog.

After I heard Mike put Mister Bunny into the box, he told us to come with him. Mike said this would be private, just the three of us. We walked to the special garden. I heard Mike dig a hole and bury Mister Bunny. "Come springtime, Tundra Girl," Mike said, "I will plant flowers here for your friend. I am very proud of what you did to make that bunny's last days special."

Tundra started to cry and I stood next to her to comfort her.

"Tundra," a familiar voice said. "You should be happy not sad. You did a very special thing for that bunny."

Tundra said, "Aunt Sandy?"

"Yes Tunny, it is me. Let me show you something very awesome. And you too, Rivers," Sandy said. "Now, both of you close your eyes and you will see Mister Bunny running in a beautiful field of clover. Do you see all those other bunnies with him? Those are his family and friends. Mister Bunny is in a better place where he is not old, hurt, or sick, and has other bunnies to play with. He is safe, Tundra. Mister Bunny is home, and you made his journey there so much better."

Sandy continued, "You tried to help a fellow fur creature, a stranger to you, Tunny. You took him in, cared for him, and kept him warm. You made sure he was not alone. You tried and that is all that really counts."

"But he died, Aunt Sandy," Tunny said. "I could not stop that."

"No Tunny, you did not let him die, and you could not stop him from dying. Mister Bunny was dying when you found him." Sandy

continued, "What you did that was so special was to prevent Mister Bunny from dying alone. You cared, and that is a very beautiful thing. He died near someone who cared for him. That, my Young Lady Dog Tundra, is very important. Mister Bunny had no family or friends when he found you. If it were not for you, Tunny, Mister Bunny would have died alone. No creature should die alone. Dying alone is a very sad thing."

"Tunny, be happy that Mister Bunny is in a better place, but more important, take comfort in the fact that you gave of yourself, you tried, and you where there for another."

Sandy continued, "Tomorrow is Christmas and you will lead the team, with your Uncle Rivers, to the orphanage and make those poor children very happy. I want you to be happy with them and not sad. Since you showed that you have the true spirit of Christmas, I will take away the sadness you are feeling, and replace it with joy and happiness."

"I have to go," Sandy said, "Thank you for making me proud of you Tundra; you are a very good dog. You are like your Uncle Rivers. You have a heart of gold. You showed everyone that you know the true meaning of this beautiful season, the 'Season of Giving'."

I heard Sandy nuzzle Tundra. I felt Sandy come close, nuzzle me and then she was gone.

It was only a few seconds after Sandy left that Tundra asked, "Uncle Rivers, did Aunt Sandy just visit us or was I dreaming?"

"Yes, Tunny that was your Aunt Sandy. She came to comfort you in your sadness by showing you all of the good things you did for Mister Bunny. Are you okay?" I asked.

"Yeah, Uncle Rivers, for some reason I do not feel sad, actually I am happy that Mister Bunny is home." Silently, I thanked Sandy for comforting Tundra.

"Come on, Uncle Rivers, we have snow to play in, and you and me will be the lead dogs tomorrow," Tundra said as she grabbed on to my collar and took me to the yard to play.

Springtime Showdown

The snow was gone. The trails dried out. The temperatures were warming and there was the scent of Mary's flowers in the air. Well, since the serious running season was over, we took short training runs to keep in shape. However, we spent most of our time relaxing and planning for the next snow season.

Both Geezer and Stryker became permanent members of our family. Geezer, being too old to run the trails became Caitlyn's constant companion. Mike fitted him with a special harness so he could lead Caitlyn. Now Caitlyn is free to roam the yard and gardens without Mike, Mary, or Randy with her.

Stryker healed completely, but with only three legs, he does not run the trails with us. However, he is still a part of our team because he rides in the sled or cart basket, barking encouragement to us. Mike said that when Stryker sits in the sled basket barking at us, he sounds like a "drill sergeant." You have to ask Mike about that. I have no idea what a "drill sergeant" is. All I know is that Mike is our musher and Stryker is now our coach. If Stryker is not with us in our yard or on the trails, he hangs out with Geezer and Caitlyn.

I heard that both Geezer and Stryker sleep in Caitlyn's bedroom. You know, it is funny how life turns out. Both Geezer and Stryker were trained to protect their humans, yet they were abandoned when they became too old or maimed. Now they have new jobs guiding and protecting Caitlyn, ironically, who is blind. Bark about a sense of purpose.

I was enjoying my happy thoughts as I heard Mike come out of the big house and walk to the kennel. Randy was with him. We knew Mike had to leave for a few days on a business trip. I heard Mike ask Randy to take Christmas, Sky, Tundra, and Stormy to Doctor Jim's for their yearly checkups. Mike suggested using the training cart so the dogs could "mush" down the road to Doctor Jim's clinic. Mike said he would take the rest of us dogs to Doctor Jim's clinic when he returns in a few days.

I knew from the excitement in Randy's voice that he was glad to do that. While Christmas is very devoted to Mike, she and her girls consider themselves Randy's team and she gets very excited when the five of them take off on a trail run.

Mike gave us all ear rubs and told us to be good while he was gone. I heard him leave the kennel for his business trip.

Randy came into the kennel and started to do his yard chores, which we all prevented him from doing. Tundra dropped tennis balls at Randy's feet coaxing Randy to toss the balls for her to chase. Nitro and Brownie had a pull rope and kept wrapping it around Randy's legs. Randy still did not get the hint that it was playtime as Sky and Stormy kept rubbing up against him for some extra ear rubs.

I heard Caitlyn, Geezer, and Stryker come out of the house as Christmas was telling the dogs to let Randy do his chores. "Work first then playtime, my Young Lady Dogs," Christmas said to them.

"Hi Randy", Caitlyn said as Christmas told me that Geezer guided Caitlyn to the kennel.

"Good morning Caitlyn," Randy replied. "You sure are up early."

"Yes, I smelled the flowers and other spring scents and figured it was a good day to get out of the house. Mary is not feeling well and may stay in bed for a while. She needs her rest to get over whatever made her sick."

"That is smart thinking on your part, Caitlyn," Randy replied. "I have some chores to do, that is, if these dogs let me do them. Then I have to run Christmas, Sky, Tundra, and Stormy to Doctor Jim's clinic." Randy asked Caitlyn, "Do you want to go for a ride?"

"No thanks, Randy". Caitlyn replied. "I think I will head over to the special garden where Sandy and Mr. Bunny are buried. The flowers smell so nice, and it is so peaceful. It is a perfect spot for reflecting."

"Yes, it is very pretty up there," Randy replied. "Just be careful. I will run the dogs past you on my way to and from Doctor Jim's clinic to make sure you are okay."

I heard Lakota sit down next to me. "Hi Rivers," Lakota said.

"Good morning Lakota," I replied. As you know, Lakota is my best friend and acts as my "eyes." He started to describe to me how Geezer was leading Caitlyn to the special garden. Caitlyn was holding on to the special harness Mike made. Geezer was on Caitlyn's right side, while Stryker walked on her left side. She made a big fuss over both dogs, telling them how handsome they were. My mind's eye could picture

Caitlyn surrounded by her buddies. She sounded a lot happier than the crying girl who ran away from the orphanage in a blizzard. I know we all are very happy that we could find her that Christmas Eve.

"You know, Rivers, you seem to find or collect dogs and humans that become our family members," Lakota said

"Gee, Lakota, I am not sure what you are driving at," I said.

"Okay," Lakota said. "Do you remember who found Christmas in the woods? Who met Geezer coming up the driveway? What about Stryker? You found him also. You met Randy in town and Caitlyn at the orphanage. Then found her in the blizzard. Did you forget Nitro, Brownie, Doc, Ugly, and me? If it had not been for you, we would never have found our forever home here with Mike and Mary."

"I never thought of it that way," I said. "Maybe I did not find you guys. Maybe, you found me."

"Okay Rivers, now you got me thinking about something that I thought I had pretty well figured out," Lakota said.

"Maybe, Lakota," I chuckled, "you are thinking way too hard."

Lakota laughed as he said, "look who is barking about thinking too hard about things."

I guess Nitro, Brownie, Doc, and Ugly must have heard us laughing because they came over to us to see what was so funny.

Ugly chuckled as he barked, "What are you guys laughing about? You know, I tell the jokes around here, and I have not told any funny ones today."

Before anyone could answer, I said, "Quiet, I hear something."

There were strange sounds coming from the side of the house where the special garden is. I heard a low growl, a dog's warning.

However, before I could say anything we all heard, "Well, look what we have here. Is that the three-legged dog we beat up a while back? Maybe we need to pick up where we left off before those two dogs and that crazy human stopped us."

Stryker replied, "Yes, you are right, I am that three-legged dog you met a few months back. However, this time, I am not hungry or cold, and I am not as weak as I was then. I think you and your friends here really need to leave now."

We heard Geezer bark next, "Look gentlemen, it is a very nice day, too nice of a day for problems. We just want to enjoy the nice day with our young friend here. So how about it if you guys leave?"

This is getting intense. Who knows how many dogs are threaten-

ing our buddies. These same dogs attacked Stryker. However, more importantly, Caitlyn is out there. We need to help them.

Nitro must have read my thoughts because he said, "We need to get out of the yard and help Caitlyn, Geezer, and Stryker."

Brownie asked, "But Nitro, how? We cannot jump the fence."

"Mike never repaired the loose boards on the back wall of the warming hut. Remember, we broke through them to bring Christmas into our yard the night we found her in the woods," Doc said.

"Okay," Nitro said. "Here is the plan. Lakota, Brownie, and I will go through those loose boards and race around the left side of house. We will come up behind the strangers. Doc, Ugly and Rivers, you guys race straight up the path between the house and the special garden. Bark like mad since we need you to occupy the attention of those bad dogs until Lakota, Brownie and I get into position."

Ugly asked how I was going find my way there since we have to run fast to make time.

I said, "That is not a problem, Ugly. Just get the pull game rope. I will be on one end, you on the other. You can guide me just like being on a neckline."

"Good idea, Rivers," Nitro said. "We are wasting time let's go."

Lakota, Nitro, and Brownie burst through the loose board and ran to the left side of the kennel. Ugly had the pull rope. He had one end and I had the other. He started to lead me out of the opening of the warming hut. We went to the right side of the kennel and Doc lead us up the path to the special garden. We wanted the strange dogs to hear us barking at them as we charged at them.

I knew where I was going once we raced through the warming hut and past the kennel. We ran like crazy and soon I heard Caitlyn yelling, "Back, back," at the strange dogs. Doc told me Stryker was out front, confronting the dogs. Geezer stayed back shielding Caitlyn with his body.

"Well, what do we have here," the leader of the dog pack said, once he saw us. "You got three other dogs to help you. One looks like he is blind. One is so small that a good wind would blow him over. And that dog with the rope in his mouth looks like some kind of circus animal."

We positioned ourselves next to Stryker. Doc said, "Please understand that your idiotic comments really do not bother us. I really must advise you that it would be in your best interest to leave. Now!"

I knew Ugly was really upset being called a circus animal. His feelings came across very clearly when he said, "My name is Ugly and I tell jokes. I would tell you one right now, but I do not believe you have the ability to comprehend anything intelligent other than the sound, 'duh'."

"Now, let me get this straight," I said. "You want to pick on a three-legged dog, a blind dog, a small dog, an old dog, and a retired racing dog. You also want to threaten a little blind girl. Sounds like the perfect thing for real tough dogs like you and your pack to do. Sorry, it is not going to happen."

"Oh, and you old has-beens are going to stop us?" The leader of the pack said.

"Sure, they are." It was Nitro. "And if you do not leave now, you will soon regret your decision to stay. This is my yard and these are my friends. That young girl over there is my human companion, and we are all dedicated to protecting her. You may think it is cool to pick on the weak, the hurt, the old, or the maimed, Pack Dog, but you and your gang are nothing more than a bunch of cowards. I think you were advised to leave."

I was not sure what was going to happen next. Remember, I have heard Nitro go into full rage. I heard Lakota tackle a human who slashed me with a knife. Brownie has always been there when things got tough. He is one tough dog who will not back down. Brownie was right by my side when I faced the wolf that hurt our friend Sunny. As I barked before, this was becoming very intense.

The pack dog leader had to make a decision here very soon. There are eight dogs here, dedicated to protecting Caitlyn and each other. The pack leader never had a chance to make his decision. I heard Christmas and her girls, with Randy, racing up the trail, blocking the pack dogs retreat. Doc told me Christmas was leading the team. I knew she would not be a very happy Husky with strangers in her yard, especially around Caitlyn. I heard her snarling, barking and growling at the pack dogs. Yep, you can say Christmas was a little bit angry. Now, the pack dogs have twelve dogs, plus a human to contend with.

"Well, Pack Dog, it appears you have a huge problem right now." I said, "Your escape route is blocked. I would be very leery of that lady dog over there leading the dog team. She does not take too kindly of strangers threatening her human. I am sure you know about getting on the bad side of lady dogs."

We all heard the zipper of the cart bag. We knew Randy was go-

ing for the rifle Mike keeps in the sled bag when we travel by cart or sled.

"I think your time has run out, Pack Dog". It was Stryker. "That young man is getting a gun. I will assure you he is an excellent shot. He will not hesitate to shoot you and your fellow pack dogs since you are a threat to his sister and his dogs." I heard the chuckle in Stryker's voice as he said. "You have only one chance, Pack Dog, and that is to run as fast you and your pack can through the brush. I promise you, we will not follow you."

Pack Dog said as he and the other dogs raced through the brush, "You may have won this battle, War Dog, but we will be back."

As the pack dogs ran through the brush, Stryker barked, "Actually, no, Pack Dog. You have just lost the war."

With that, Doc told me Stryker pulled on a rope he picked by the brush. "Quick, help me pull this rope," Stryker said.

As we pulled on the rope, I heard a gate groan as it started to close. Then I heard the sound of a latch locking on a fence post.

Before I could ask, Stryker said, "There is some kind of fenced-in area on the other side of that gate. You can hardly see it since there is a lot of brush and bramble hiding the fence. I explored it and it is solid. It will make a good holding pen for our 'guests'."

I heard Randy say, "Okay, everyone in line. Walk back to the kennel." Lakota came up beside me and said that all the dogs were following Randy and the team back to the kennel. He nudged me into the line of dogs following Randy. Lakota told me that Stryker and Geezer were guiding Caitlyn back to the house.

Once we were in the kennel, Randy took off the other dogs' harnesses and put them in the kennel with us. He got us all fresh water and gave us some treats. Randy said he was going to call animal control and ask them to come and get the Pack Dogs from their "guest quarters".

A short time later, I heard a truck come up the driveway. Stormy told me that Mary and Randy came out of the house to talk to the driver of the truck. I heard them talk about the stray dogs. Randy told the driver that he saw the strays in the pen and closed the gate on them. Randy knew that there was no point in going into any detail about this. The driver would never believe what we did.

Later that evening, Geezer and Stryker came out to visit us in the kennel. Geezer thanked us for helping them. Nitro said, "We are all family here in this kennel. Our job, like yours, is to take care of our humans. I notice that neither of you two backed down from the pack dogs. You were outnumbered three dogs to one."

Stryker answered, "We could not back down, not with Miss Caitlyn in danger. To be honest, I was hoping I could hold off the dogs while Geezer got Miss Caitlyn to safety. I never imagined you would get out of the kennel and come to help us. It was a great plan that you had, cutting off their retreat, while distracting them. Miss Christmas sure got nasty with the pack dog leader."

"Yes, she sure did," I replied. "Christmas considers Caitlyn one of her 'babies'. I guess she saw one of her 'babies' in danger out there. Christmas is a force to be reckoned with if she wants to be."

Stryker said, "Miss Tundra, Sky, and Stormy seem to share their mother's protective nature. I really would not want any of them, or you guys for that matter, upset with me." Stryker continued, "I have been meaning to ask you, Rivers. I notice Miss Christmas and her lady dogs call you and the other dogs 'Uncle'. Are you related?"

"No, Stryker," I said, "we are not. After we found Christmas, we raised and protected her. Therefore, we became her 'Uncles'. The same is true for her girls." I added, "By the way, Stryker, you do not need to call the girls 'Miss'. You are family here. You do not have to be so formal."

"Family," Stryker sighed, "I never had any that I can remember. My military handler was my family, and I guess there were brothers and sisters in the litter I came from. But, I really never had any family, like you all have here."

"Well, Stryker, you really need to try and get use to it." Christmas said as she joined us, "You are family now, especially after protecting Caitlyn like you did. Uncle Rivers is right. Please call me Christmas, and my girls Sky, Tundra, and Stormy. They will call you Uncle Stryker because you are older than they are. It is a respect thing, right Uncle Rivers?"

"Right, Miss Christmas," I said chuckling.

Do You Believe In Miracles?

What is that sound I hear? It sounds like caroling. Yes, Christmas caroling! That means it is Christmas time again! Stormy was very excited. She told me Mike was putting the big Santa on the roof, while Randy strung bright colored lights all around the house. Every once in a while, I would get a whiff of the great stuff Mary and Caitlyn were cooking for the holidays. I never developed a taste for human food, but the terrific smells and scents that came from Mary's kitchen might change my mind about it, especially turkey.

Stormy told me the twinkling lights reflected beautifully on the snow. Yes, I could picture the twinkling lights in my mind's eye. I heard all of the dogs in the kennel. They were doing their kennel things. Ugly told jokes to Brownie and Doc, while Nitro barked trail stories to Tundra and Sky, as their Momma Christmas listened. Nitro can bark some very tall trail tales.

I was "seeing" and enjoying all of this activity in my mind's eye, when I noticed that I did not hear Lakota. Normally, he would be walking with me as my "eyes" or talking with Doc and Nitro, or Stryker and Geezer if they were in the yard. So where was Lakota? He loves this time of year, enjoying the decorations and especially going to the orphanage and playing with the children while Mike plays 'Santa'."

I asked Stormy, "Do you see Lakota?"

"No Uncle Rivers, I do not see him with the other dogs. Maybe he is outside the kennel with Mike and Randy. Sometimes Mike lets Lakota wander out there with Stryker and Geezer," Stormy replied.

We walked over to the gate so Stormy could get a better view of the outside yard. "I do not see him with Stryker or Geezer, Uncle Rivers. Maybe he is in his doghouse," Stormy said. "Do you want me to walk with you to it?"

I replied, "No thanks, Stormy. I can get to Lakota's house by myself. You can go and listen to Ugly's jokes or Nitro's stories, if you want."

"You sure, Uncle Rivers? I do not mind walking with you," Stormy said.

"Go have some fun, Stormy. I can make it to Lakota's doghouse," I replied.

"Okay Uncle Rivers. See ya," Stormy said as I heard her scamper off in the direction of Nitro and her sisters.

It was easy for me to find Lakota's doghouse since it is next to mine. As I walked closer to his house, I smelled the food we had for chow. I found his food bowl, still full of chow. Interesting, I thought. Lakota never misses a meal.

As I stuck my head into the opening of Lakota's doghouse, I heard him breathing. I did not hear the deep even breathing of a good sleep, but only the shallow sound of a very tired dog. Concerned, I asked, "Lakota, are you okay?"

"Hi, Rivers," Lakota answered, but I knew I had startled him. "Yes, I am okay, just tired."

"Your food bowl is full of chow Lakota, you did not eat. That is not like you," I said.

"I just was not hungry," he said. "I was very tired after the fun run and I just wanted to rest."

"That fun run was not that long, Lakota. It should not have made you so tired that you were too exhausted to eat," I replied. "What is wrong?"

"Rivers, I am okay. Really, I am fine. Sometimes I just feel my age. I will be okay for the trip to the orphanage. I just need a good night's sleep," Lakota said.

"All right, I will keep an eye on you when we run the trails tomorrow," I said.

I heard a faint chuckle in Lakota's bark when he said, "I am sure you will, Rivers. Good night, my friend."

I heard him start to snore as I walked back to the other dogs. Yes, I was concerned, but it is best to keep my concerns to myself. I am sure that Lakota will be okay.

I can sleep through thunder, or the screeching of the eagles in the trees by our yard. However, sleep is impossible when Mike starts banging on the food bucket and sings, "Wake up, sleepy heads, get your fannies out of bed. It is chow time!"

After I finished eating, I walked over to Lakota's doghouse to see how he was doing. Mike was standing by the doghouse. I sniffed Lakota's food bowl and it was still full. One missed meal I can accept, but not

two in a row. Something was wrong. Mike must have been reading my mind because I heard him say, "Lakota, are you okay?"

I felt Stormy come up beside me and she whispered into my ear that Lakota did not look well. Mike was checking him out. Stormy told me that Mike looked into Lakota's mouth and checked his gums for the right color. Then Mike checked Lakota's paws for any problems. "Your eyes are clear, no foul odor from your mouth, and your paws are okay. What is wrong Lakota?" Mike asked, "How come you are not eating?"

Then Stormy told me that Mike ran his hands all over Lakota's back and sides, but stopped when he touched Lakota's tummy. "Hmm, your tummy is a bit hard Lakota," Mike said. "I think we need to go see Doctor Jim."

Stormy told me that Mike went to the warming hut and came back with a leash in his hand. He clipped the leash onto Lakota and they started walking to the kennel gate. Randy came out of the house and Mike said to Randy, "I am taking Lakota to see Doctor Jim. Lakota has not been eating and his tummy is very hard. It could be a blockage or a tumor. Doctor Jim will find out for sure." Mike continued, "I fed all of the dogs. Would you mind picking up the dog bowls and giving them fresh water? I think we will take a break from the fun run today."

"Sure Mike," Randy said. Stormy told me that Randy gave Lakota a few ear rubs before Mike put Lakota into the front of the truck. I sat down by the gate to wait for Mike to bring Lakota back from Doctor Jim's clinic.

When Mike returned, I jumped up to greet my best friend. However, Lakota was not with Mike. Where is Lakota?

I heard Randy race over to the gate and ask Mike, "Where is Lakota?"

Mike replied in a somber tone, "Doctor Jim said that Lakota has a large tumor by his spleen. Doctor Jim is removing it now. I will pick up Lakota later today. Doctor Jim will run some tests to determine if the tumor is cancerous."

Randy exclaimed, "Cancer! I did not know dogs could get cancer."

"Yes," Mike said. "Besides broken bones, dogs suffer from many of the same health problems we humans do. For example, Rivers lost his sight to Glaucoma and cataracts. Both are common in humans."

Mike continued, "Lakota can live without a spleen, but if the spleen is cancerous, then his chances would not be too good. The problem is that Doctor Jim must cut out all of the cancer cells. That would be very difficult if the spleen ruptured. It would be very easy for the cancer to spread."

"Lakota will come home later today no matter what Doctor Jim finds inside him," Mike said. "We need to get the warming hut ready for him."

I heard them walk to the warming hut. I was barkless. My best friend may be very sick. I was becoming very sad and angry. This is not fair to Lakota. He is a good dog, a great friend, and does not deserve to be sick. What a horrible thing to happen to Lakota at Christmas time.

I guess the other dogs heard Mike talking to Randy and came over to be with me. They were all shocked as I was, and like me, upset. Lakota is our friend, part of our team, and our family.

"Momma," Tundra asked, "Is Uncle Lakota going to cross the Rainbow Bridge?"

"I do not know, Tunny." Christmas said. "I hope not."

"Mike will not let that happen," I said gruffly.

"Rivers, you should not say that," Doc said. "Mike does not have the power to cure something as bad as cancer. You know that. It is not fair to give Tunny false hope."

"I am very sorry, Tundra. I should not have said that to you. I am very upset about Lakota. He has been my best friend for a very long time," I said. "Doc is right. No human can stop our journey when our time comes to cross the Bridge. Our human companions can only make our journey easier."

I heard Tunny start to cry as well as her sisters, Sky and Stormy. I heard their Mother, Christmas, crying also. Lakota is a great "uncle" to all of them.

I was angry with myself for upsetting the young dogs. I should have known better. I guess my own feelings got in the way of my better judgment.

"There is a truck coming up the driveway," I barked. "It sounds like Doctor Jim's mobile clinic."

"You are right, Rivers," Ugly said. "I hope Doctor Jim is bringing Lakota home and has some good news for us."

Stormy told me that Mike came out of the big house just as Doctor Jim was getting out of his truck.

"Mike," Doctor Jim said, "I brought Lakota home for you. He did very well in the surgery."

Stormy told me that Mike walked over to where Doctor Jim was standing by his truck. All of the dogs in our yard were standing by the gate, eagerly waiting for the news.

"The tumor was not in the spleen, but in one of Lakota's kidneys. I removed the kidney. That is the good news. The bad news is that the tumor was cancerous. However, I think I cut it all out since I did not find cancer cells anywhere else in the kidney area. Lakota can live very well with only one kidney."

Doctor Jim continued, "Mike, Lakota is much older than we first thought. Therefore, my first concern is that he recovers from the surgery, and his remaining kidney picks up the load of the removed kidney. It will take some time for him to get his strength back. After that, it is a matter of making sure he does not lose too much weight."

"One last thing Mike," Doctor Jim said. "I had to shave much of his tummy hair off to do the surgery. He cannot stay outside for a long time in very cold weather or else his bare skin will get frostbite. He should get all of his fur back in 4 months or so."

Mike replied, "Thanks Doctor Jim. I figured you would shave him for the surgery so we prepared the warming hut for him. He will stay in there with one or two of his buddies to keep him company. When do you want to see Lakota again?"

"I need to remove the stitches in about 10 days. He may not eat tonight. The medicine I gave him to sedate him for the surgery should wear off very soon. If he does not start eating, drinking, and peeing normally by morning, please give me a call. But honestly, Mike, if he does not start by tomorrow night, then his chances for recovery would be very slim."

All of us were barkless. Lakota is very sick and may not live. Oh no!

Stormy told me that Doctor Jim and Mike walked to the back of the truck. They got Lakota out and, as he started walking towards the kennel, he stumbled. Mike gently picked him up, carried him into the yard, and then to the warming hut. We all followed.

Stormy told me Mike placed Lakota on a big bed of straw and put a blanket over him. Mike wet his fingers in the bowl of water that was on the floor ready if wanted a drink. Mike put his wet fingers to Lakota's mouth. Stormy told me that Lakota licked Mike's fingers.

"Okay, Team, you heard Doctor Jim. Lakota needs his rest. Go out to the yard." I heard Christmas move next to me and told me all the dogs sat down by Lakota. So did Christmas. I remained standing. Like my teammates, I was not leaving Lakota alone.

"I do not believe this," Doctor Jim said. "I never saw any of your dogs disobey you, Mike. They all sat down except for Rivers. How come they disobeyed you?"

"Doctor Jim, they are just being family," Mike said. "Just like human families cling together during tragedies, these dogs are doing the same thing. They stand by each other. They take care of each other and protect each other. They run like a team, but live like a family." Mike continued, "They will not leave Lakota. They will stay with him until he gets well or..." Mike's voice grew softer as he spoke those words.

Doctor Jim replied, "This is Christmas time, Mike, and it always seems that interesting things happen at your kennel during this time of the year. Maybe we will witness another miracle."

"Yes," Mike said, "that would be real nice, Doctor Jim."

I heard Doctor Jim and Mike leave the warming hut. We were all silent, lost in our own thoughts.

When Mike returned to the warming hut, Christmas told me that he had the food bucket. It must be chow time. "Okay, Team, go to the yard for chow. When you finish eating, you may come back into the warming hut."

This time, we all went to the yard as Mike told us to do. Christmas told me that when she looked around to see Lakota, Mike was knelling down next to him giving him a good ear rub. He also put a bowl of food down for him. I heard Mike whisper to Lakota, "Okay, Buddy, you can do this. You can win this race and beat this cancer. I'm pulling for ya."

After we ate, we all went back into the warming hut. Lakota was awake but not in a happy mood. He asked that we all leave except for Nitro and me.

"I do not think I will make it, I feel so tired and weak. I do not want the rest of the team to see me like this," Lakota said.

"Are you giving up on us, Lakota?" It was Nitro. "The Lakota I knew, my teammate, never gave up. He was right there by my side when that bear tried to get over the fence in our yard. My teammate, Lakota, helped me stop the bad human who tried to hurt Mike when Mike had a broken arm. My teammate, Lakota, was right by my side and faced down those dogs that wanted to hurt Caitlyn, Geezer, and Stryker. My teammate Lakota's wisdom helped prevent trouble, but he never backed away from it when it came looking for him." Nitro demanded, "Where is my teammate Lakota now?"

I did not give Lakota time to answer. "The dogs you asked to leave are your teammates and friends. Most importantly, Lakota, they are your family. They want to be with you because you need us now. If

59

it is your time to cross the Bridge, then allow your family to be with you when you start your journey," I said. "A very dear friend of mine told me that the power to heal comes from within us. Lakota, you have much to live for. I do not believe you are willing to let life go without a fight."

Lakota answered, "I am very tired, please go. I want to be alone."

"Very well, Lakota," Nitro replied. "We will let you rest, but we will not leave you alone. All of the dogs in the yard want to be here with you, and I will not stop them. They have a right to be here with you because they are your teammates, your friends, and your family. You may have given up, Lakota, but we have not given up on you."

I added, "Have you forgotten Mike? Has he ever given up on you or any other of your teammates?"

Nitro told me that Lakota closed his eyes and went to sleep. Nitro's talk surprised me. I would expect Doc or maybe Christmas to say something like that to Lakota. However, hearing it from rough and tough Nitro was amazing. Yes, wonders never cease to amaze me.

All the dogs returned from the yard and settled in to sleep in the warming hut with Lakota. Mike came by to check on all of us. He knelt down next to Lakota. Sky told me that Mike stretched out next to Lakota and cradled Lakota in his arms. Mike talked very softly to Lakota, telling him what a good dog he was and how proud he was of him. Mike told Lakota that he would take Lakota to the orphanage to spend Christmas with the poor children. Mike knew how much Lakota enjoyed visiting the children. He told Lakota that Mary was making something very special for Lakota's Christmas chow.

After a while, Mike stood up and left. Nature was calling me so I walked with Mike out of the warming hut to the yard. Mike gave me a great ear rub as he asked, "You okay, Rivers?"

After the ear rub, I headed to my favorite spot in the yard. I heard Mike open the kennel gate to go to the big house. As I walked back to the hut, I felt her walking besides me and asked. "Sandy is that you?"

"Sure is, Rivers. I am here to have a little chat with your buddy Lakota," Sandy replied.

I asked Sandy, "Does he believe you are his Guardian Angel Dog?"

"Kind of," Sandy answered. "Lakota has doubts. He is so grounded in reality that he does not believe in what he cannot see, hear, touch, or smell. However, his inner self, the part hidden by his reality side,

secretly wishes he could believe in miracles and have the vivid dreams you do. Of course, his reality side prevents that. Tonight, he will see a miracle and have vivid dreams, which may make a difference in his attitude towards his battle with this cancer." When she finished, Sandy lead me back to the warming hut.

No dog stirred as we walked into the warming hut.

No dog moved as we walked to where Lakota was sleeping.

No dog woke when Sandy barked, "Lakota, wake up!"

I saw Lakota's eyes open as he raised his head from his bed of straw. Wait a minute, I cannot see.

"Rivers, for the next few moments you will see what is going on. That is my Christmas gift to you," Sandy said.

"Lakota, do you see me." Sandy asked, "Do you know who I am?"

"Sandy! It cannot be. You died protecting Christmas and her babies from the rouge wolf," Lakota said.

"Well, Lakota, you cannot be that far gone if you remember that." Sandy asked, "Who do you see standing next to me, right in front of you?"

I see a dog that looks like a young Sandy standing next to Rivers. Rivers, is that you? Your eyes look so different," Lakota said.

"Yes, Lakota, it is me, Rivers, and my eyes do look different because I can see, but only for a short while. It is my Christmas gift from Sandy," I replied.

"But, Sandy died and you are blind." Lakota asked, "How can this be?"

"Miracles," Sandy said. "Life is full of them, if only you believe in them. I am here to give you a Christmas gift, Lakota. The gift is to dream as Rivers dreams. However, this gift will only work if you believe in miracles." Sandy continued, "Now Lakota, you will get well, and you will go to the orphanage tomorrow, and I do not want to hear any more of this 'I am tired and giving up' stuff. You understand me, Mister Lakota?"

Lakota replied, "As bossy as you are, Lady Dog, you must be Sandy."

"Good," Sandy said. "Now let me kiss my babies and give them and my other dogs their Christmas gifts."

As we left Lakota, I asked Sandy, "Are you going to visit with Mike?"

"The answer to that question is within your own heart, Rivers; you do not have to ask since you already know the answer," Sandy replied.

I watched her kiss Stormy, Sky and Tundra. She nuzzled with

Christmas and touched the paw of each dog in the hut. When she came to Nitro, she sat for a moment by him as if she was talking to him. She looked back at me, winked, and was gone.

Darkness surrounded me again as I stretched out next to my best friend, Lakota. I drifted into a very deep sleep.

Bang. Bang. Bang, and then, "Hey you sleepy heads, get your fannies out of bed. It is chow time!" Mike and his daily wakeup screech do drive the sweet dreams from a sleeping dog's head.

"Hey Rivers," it was Mike. "Are you going to join us for chow out here in the yard? Lakota is waiting of you."

Lakota is in the yard! Wow, great, I thought as I raced out to the yard.

"Rivers, I had the greatest dream," Lakota told me as I came up to him in the yard. He was very excited as he continued, "I had a great dream, which had to be as vivid as you told me your dreams are. I never had a dream that seemed so real. Wow, I saw Sandy and you could see and..."

I interrupted him asking, "Are you sure it was a dream?"

Lakota asked, "What do you mean? It had to be a dream." He continued. "Sandy crossed the bridge and you cannot see."

I replied, "Yesterday you were weak and tired. You did not want the other dogs near you. You gave up. The surgery wore you out and you gave up the fight with this cancer. This morning you are out here in the yard, drinking, eating, and answering nature's callings; a very different dog. Sounds like a miracle to me."

Lakota asked, "Miracle? Sandy used that word. She said I had to believe in miracles in order for..."

I finished his words. "...your gift to work. Sandy's gift to you was the gift to dream as vividly as I do."

"Yes, Sandy did say those exact words," Lakota replied. "Rivers, how did you know what she said?"

"Because, Lakota, I believe in miracles," I replied.

Now, Lakota is a thinker and I just knew he would be thinking about what I just said to him for a long while.

I heard Mike come out of the warming hut. "Well Lakota, since you are up and about, I think you should go to the orphanage with us. I have a dog coat for you that will cover your tummy. I am sure you do not want to pass up a free ride in the basket."

Then, Mike asked Lakota, "Well, Buddy, do you want to go?"

With a mighty bark, Lakota's answer was yes!

Earthquake!

We were returning from a great overnight trail run and camp out. The weather had been perfect. A Husky could not ask for any better trail conditions.

Mike had Stormy and Tundra in the lead position with Christmas and Sky directly behind them in the swing position. I could hear Christmas barking encouragement to her babies, Sky, Stormy, and Tundra. Babies? These babies were growing up to be wonderful lady dogs. Wow, I thought, they were just babies yesterday, now they are young adult Huskies.

Lakota and I were in the wheel position. Mike likes to keep me in the wheel position with Lakota as my teammate, since Lakota and I have been together for a long time. Lakota is very good at being my "seeing eye dog." We work together as a finely tuned team. Yep, you may consider us professional grade wheel dogs.

In front of us were Nitro and Brownie. Nitro is our biggest teammate, he is also fearless and the first one to protect the team or Mike. Brownie is our fastest dog, but many times, speedy Stormy has given Brownie a run for his dog biscuits. Brownie and Nitro are buddies. They normally run together as teammates. Like Nitro, Brownie is also brave and ready to jump in to help when necessary. Mike likes to run Brownie with Nitro since Nitro tends to slow Brownie down so Brownie does not outrun the team.

Next were Doc and Ugly. Doc is the smallest, but smartest dog on our team. He is our leader and taught all of us to be lead dogs. Well, not me, but Mike did teach me to lead by listening to his voice commands. While I love being the lead dog, it is more fun when the other dogs lead. They are so much better at it than I am. You can say that I just enjoy cruising along in the wheel dog position.

Running with Doc was Ugly. Ugly is not really an ugly dog. Ugly, according to the lady dogs on our team, is a very handsome Husky. Like the rest of us, Ugly can lead the team, run in the wheel position,

or be a great team dog. He loves to bark jokes and knows when we need a good one.

We were all just trotting along, enjoying the leisurely pace, being together, and happy to be with Mike. Mike has a great bond with all of us and we all are very devoted to him, especially Christmas. Ever since Sandy, Mike's beloved housedog died, Christmas seldom leaves Mike's side when he is with us.

I guess I was just lost in my thoughts about my buddies and Sandy when Lakota said to me, "Rivers, your ears are twitching".

Before I could answer him, I felt the ground move under my paws. It was very gentle at first, but the movement grew in intensity.

"The ground is shaking, Momma," Sky said.

Christmas calmly replied, "It is an earthquake, Sky Honey. "Just keep running and follow Mike's commands."

"We are in an open field. I bet Mike will stop the team here," Nitro said.

"Team, stop. Team, sit," Mike commanded.

We all sat on the ground as it rocked and rolled underneath us. Then all of a sudden, it stopped.

Wow, I thought, that was a strong earthquake. I hope Mary, Caitlyn, and Randy are okay. I heard Mike unzip something. Lakota told me Mike unzipped the pocket to his parka and pulled out his cell phone.

"Mary," Mike said, "are you guys okay? Did the earthquake do any damage"? Mike paused and then said, "Good, we are all okay. I stopped the team in an open field. I do not see any crevices in the ground or downed trees."

That surprised me, I thought, since the quake felt very strong.

"I am going to run the team past the orphanage and see how they are doing," Mike said. "I will call you from there. Bye".

Mike told us to stand tall and gave us the command to start running down the trail. Lakota told me the trail was clear. There were no trees down or anything blocking our way. The snow was good and allowed Mike to run us at top speed to the orphanage.

As we were getting close to the orphanage, I heard the sound of children crying.

"Holy Moly!" I heard Mike say as Lakota told me we were entering the orphanage's front yard.

I asked anxiously Lakota, "What do you see?"

"Rivers," Lakota answered. "The earthquake destroyed the orphanage! There is nothing left but a big pile of rubble. However, it looks like the children are okay."

"Whoa," Mike commanded. I heard him plant the snow hook. "Team sit," was Mike's next command.

Lakota told me that Mrs. Astor, the woman who takes care of the children at the orphanage, came over to Mike. I heard her crying.

"Mike, the orphanage is destroyed. What will I do? The children..."

Mike cut her short. "Take it easy, Mrs. Astor, first things first. Have you shut off the gas supply?"

She told Mike no and then Mike replied, "Let me take care of that first to prevent a fire or explosion." Calmly, Mike continued, "Meanwhile, please get the sleeping bag out of my sled bag, and wrap it around the smaller children. Use my parka for some of the other children. Have the children that you cannot wrap in the sleeping bag or parka cuddle with the dogs to keep warm."

I heard Mike rush off as Lakota told me that Mrs. Astor opened the sled bag and took out the sleeping bag. Lakota told me that several of the children cuddled with us to keep warm, while others bunched together, wrapped in Mike's parka.

When Mike returned he said, "I turned the gas, electricity, and water off." Next, Lakota told me that Mike took the cell phone out of his pocket. "Mary, the orphanage is totally destroyed. Have Randy load up the trailer with some blankets and coats, and bring it here with the four-wheeler. You and Caitlyn bring one of the trucks down here to get the rest of the children. We are moving them to our place. Also, please call the troopers and tell them what has happened here. I am sure that they will be very busy. Tell them there are no casualties and that we have it under control for the time being."

Soon, I heard the four-wheeler. Lakota told me Randy parked it by our sled.

"Hi Randy," Mike said. "Please start giving the blankets and coats to the children. When you are done, take the four biggest boys with you in the trailer and head back to the kennel. The older boys will help you get the warming hut set up as temporary living quarters."

Randy said, "Okay. Mary should be here shortly. According to the radio, the quake did some damage, but most of it was located south of the orphanage." Randy continued. "There are just two collapsed buildings and there is no road damage. Mary called the troopers and they will send help when they can." Randy added, "Our emergency

generator kicked in since the power went out. We have gas and water. I did not notice any damage to the house or sheds."

"Great," Mike said. "You better get going. We need to get the children settled. I am sure they are very upset. They have so little, and now they have nothing." I detected much sadness in Mike's voice.

Lakota told me that Randy passed out the coats and blankets. He gathered the four boys and took them off in the trailer. The boys sat in the trailer. No sooner did Randy leave for our home, when Mary and Caitlyn showed up with the truck.

"Hi, Hon," Mary said. They chatted for a few moments before Mary asked Mike, "What do you want me to do?"

Mike told her that Randy took four boys with him back to the kennel to set up the warming hut as temporary living quarters for the children. Mike told Mary to take Mrs. Astor and the remaining children back to the kennel in the truck. Put the boys in the warming hut. Mrs. Astor can stay in our guest bedroom while the girls can do a "sleepover" with Caitlyn in her room.

Mary asked, "Mike how long do you think they will be staying with us?"

"Until we rebuild the orphanage," Mike said.

"We rebuild the...," Mary started to say.

"Yes," Mike said, cutting her short. "I am making it my project, my job. I was getting a bit bored being retired."

"Gee Mike," Mary said, "how come life is always an adventure with you?"

I heard Mike chuckle as he asked, "Would you want it any other way than an adventure?"

Aftershocks

Chaos is scary, especially for a blind dog. However, organized chaos can be interesting. Life at the "Howlin' Rivers' Home" soon became planned chaos. The comfort of teamwork soon replaced the adversity of disaster.

The boys, including Randy, "camped out" in the warming hut. Since Randy was the oldest boy, the other boys soon considered Randy their "lead dog." Randy, with Mike, taught the boys how to care for us dogs and actually be "dog handlers" for us. Did we mind the extra hands caring for us? Nope, especially after we trained the boys in the finer points of giving us ear rubs. The boys were very excited when we took them on trail runs. The girls were also excited about our trail runs. However, they were more interested with hanging out with Caitlyn since Caitlyn is an orphanage alumnus.

Now, according to Geezer and Stryker, the girls did "sleepovers" in Caitlyn's room. Geezer told me that the girls were having a fun time, and he enjoyed them cuddling with him. According to Lakota, Geezer is big enough for all the girls to cuddle with him at the same time. He was a guard dog, right? You would not believe that he was a guard dog by the way he loves playing with the children.

Mike moved Stryker into the warming hut with the boys. I think I heard Mike chuckle when he said Stryker would probably enjoy the "camp outs" rather than the "sleepovers." Did Stryker object to the move? Not one bit.

Adversity breeds strength. As our "family" learned to deal with the cramped conditions, we all grew stronger as a team. The boys behaved very well and became very good at doing what they called their "dog chores", while caring for us, "their" dogs.

The older children went to school as normal. The school bus stopped to pick them up at the front of our driveway. Geezer told me the children, who were too young to go to school, were preschooled by Mary, Mrs. Astor, and surprisingly, by Caitlyn.

The confusion and chaos caused by the earthquake that destroyed

the orphanage soon changed to a normal, well-tuned way of life. Surprisingly, we dogs heard no complaints, or whining from any of the children. Not even from the younger ones.

Each night after all the children were asleep, Mike would visit us in the yard. Sometimes, Mary would come with Mike. One evening, Mrs. Astor joined us.

"Mike and Mary," Mrs. Astor said. "How will the children and I ever thank you for all you have done. Without your help, these children would have been sent to..." Mrs. Astor paused, "who knows where. It just amazes me how well behaved the children have been and so willing to help."

Mary said, "We are very happy to help. By the way, have you heard from your insurance company about rebuilding the orphanage?"

"Yes," Mrs. Astor said. "My insurance policy did not cover earthquakes. I just could not afford the extra coverage. It is very expensive. And," Mrs. Astor paused, "I have no way to rebuild the orphanage. In fact, the monthly mortgage payment is due very soon and I do not have the money to pay it."

Mike interrupted her. "No insurance to rebuild and a monthly mortgage payment due soon. Well, talk about a heavy load."

Mrs. Astor continued. "There is more. If I do not make the payment, or I am late with it, the bank will want full payment of my mortgage loan. In the past, the bank was very understanding. The bank just asked me to call them if I needed to make a late payment, and then make the payment when I could. I was never more than a few days late. Fortunately, right now, I am not behind with any of the payments.

Mrs. Astor continued. "That was until recently. A few weeks ago, a land developer named Mister Manhow visited me. He wanted to buy the land the orphanage stood on. I refused, of course, because without the orphanage, where would the children go? I could not just leave them, could I?"

"A few days after Mister Manhow's visit at the orphanage, a new person started handling my loan at the bank. His name was Mister Vandergoat. He told me if I was late with one more payment, he would immediately call in my loan. Mister Vandergoat is not a very nice person. He is really rude, too."

Mike said, "I will pay the bank three months of payments. That will stop them from starting any kind of foreclosure action. Mean-

while, we need to look at a fund raiser to pay off the loan and rebuild the orphanage."

Mike to the rescue, I thought as I heard, "Mike, I see that twinkle in your eye," Mary said. "You are hatching a plan in that brain of yours. What is it?"

Mike said, "The big race is coming up. The team and I will run it. We cannot win, but we can race for donations. People can pledge whatever they want for each mile of the race we complete. We will call it 'Paw Pledges'."

"Mike, you need twelve dogs to start the race," Mary said. "Your team only has ten. Besides that, Rivers is blind, and Lakota has only one kidney."

Mike said, "Yes, Mary, you make several very good points. However, Rivers and Lakota have run this race before. Being blind never stopped Rivers from running. Lakota, well, I know his desire, and he will want to go. Besides, I can drop him after the start if he shows any signs that he is not up to running." Mike continued, "Doctor Jim's Sunny can run with us. She has been training with us. And I know I can borrow Fin. He has been training with a friend of mine." Mike sounded very excited when he said, "We have been training. We have been running distances. I can think of no better reason to do this. This can work, it is doable!"

Mary said, "Mike, you have never raced."

Mike replied, "True, but I have helped others. Besides, Mary, we are not racing. All we really would be doing is a long trail run with many campouts."

Mary said, "You are too old."

Mike he replied, "I am younger than others who have completed this race."

Mary said, "The male dogs are too old." Hmm, I wondered, is Mary calling us old?

Mike laughed as he replied, "Age is just a figment of your imagination, nothing more than an indicator of time passed. It is a done deal." Mike said, "The team and I will race to raise money for the rebuilding the orphanage."

"Hey gang, did you hear that? We race again," I said.

Lakota added, "Like Mike said, you bet I want to go. I will not let having only one kidney stop me from running this race with my Mike!"

Nitro, "It is about time. There really is no retirement for a racing sled dog."

Brownie, "You are so right, Nitro. We are way too young to retire."

Ugly, "I cannot wait to do my 'Ugly Jig' at the finish line."

Doc reminded us, "This race is for the children, guys, not for us. However, it sure will be fun to race together as a team once again. And with Mike no less, what better adventure could we ask for?"

Christmas asked her girls, "What do you think about this my Young Lady Dogs? Are you up for another race?"

Sky replied, "You bet, Momma! Running this race with Mike will be awesome."

Tundra said, "Absolutely! I am ready to go right now."

Stormy added. "I cannot wait, Momma! It is going to be hard to wait until race time."

And, I thought my racing days were over. Life is just full of surprises and challenges.

The Seeds of Adventure

Lakota told me that Mike drove the team up the driveway. He then gave us the stop command, and parked our sled by our kennel. Stryker was in the basket, barking encouragement to us. After I heard Mike set the snow hook, I heard him step off the sled runners. Lakota told me that Mike then opened the gate to our yard.

I heard Stryker jump out of the sled basket. Lakota told me Stryker stretched a bit, and then walked up and down the team, telling us how good we looked on the trails today. I am not sure how much Stryker really knows about mushing, but we always appreciate his barks of praise. He always makes us feel great.

Surprisingly, Geezer was in the yard, which meant that Caitlin was not home. She must be out with Mary. With Randy and the older orphanage children in school, seeing Geezer in the yard probably meant Mrs. Astor was napping with the very young children in the big house.

I overheard Geezer confirm my assumptions with Stryker. Lakota told me Mike started to take the team off the gang line. Mike would normally take the wheel dogs, in this case, Lakota and me, off the gang line first. However, when Mike heard the vehicle drive up the driveway, he moved to the next dogs in line, which were Nitro and Brownie.

I did not recognize the sound of the vehicle or the voices of the humans in it. Hmmm…was that the reason why my neck hairs were bristling? Why did I hear Christmas, one of our lead dogs, leading the team back around Mike? Why were Nitro, Brownie, Stryker, and Geezer staying very close to Mike? A dog can sense danger. Is Mike in danger? If so, does Mike know it?

"Mister Dillingham?" I heard a human ask as Lakota told me that one of the humans got out of the vehicle.

"Yes," Mike said. "Is there something I can do for you?"

Lakota told me that Christmas moved the dogs behind where Nitro and Brownie were sitting next to Mike. Lakota also told me that

Geezer and Stryker sat in front of Mike. Therefore, anyone trying to get to Mike would have to go over a dog or two.

"My name is Mister Jacob Manhow of the JacMan Group and I have a business proposition for you," the human said. "I am allergic to dogs, Mister Dillingham, would you mind if we talked away from your team?"

"Sure," Mike said, as Lakota told me that Mike stepped around the dogs and walked near the gate to our yard. "But I have chores to do and I need to take care of my dogs," Mike said with a very mischievous, but leery tone in his voice, "I am sure they are very hungry after running the trails this morning."

Lakota told me that all of the dogs started moving towards Mike. "Stay. Sit," Mike commanded. Lakota told me all the dogs sat except Stryker. He continued to walk towards Mike. Lakota said that Stryker was limping.

"Stryker," I asked. "Are you hurt?"

"No, Rivers," Stryker replied. "I do not trust this human and I want to be by Mike in case there is a problem." Stryker continued, "Nitro, those other humans in the vehicle may have weapons. Be careful."

I asked Lakota if Mike has his gun on him. Besides the big gun Mike keeps in the sled bag, he normally carries a small one on his belt when we are on the trails. Lakota told me he did see it, but that was when Mike was about to take us off the gang line. He cannot see the gun now because Mike's parka is blocking his view.

"Excuse me, Mister Manhow. As you can see, my dog is limping. I need to tend to him. I hope you do not mind if I do that while we talk." Mike asked, "Do you?"

"Ah, well, I... well to get to the point," Mister Manhow said.

"Yes, please do get to the point, Mister Manhow," Mike said. "I have a lot of chores to do. I am a very busy man these days."

"Yes, I understand." Mister Manhow replied and then asked, "Well, how much money do you want for not running the big race to Nome?"

Lakota told me that Mike stood up since he knelt down to check out Stryker's paw. Stryker meanwhile positioned himself in front of Mike, facing Mister Manhow. I sensed the rest of the dogs tense up. We wondered if Mike would take the money not to run the race.

"$15 million," Mike answered with no hesitation.

Mister Manhow exclaimed, "That is absurd, Mister Dillingham!"

"Yep, I know that and so is your feeble attempt to bribe me not to run this race," Mike answered. "That orphanage will be rebuilt and nothing will stop that from happening." Mike continued, "I know you are the land developer who pressured the bank to foreclose on Mrs. Astor's orphanage."

"And you are the one who paid her mortgage for three months." Mister Manhow countered. "I can wait. As you know, accidents happen and I am very confident you will have one."

Oops, not a nice thing to say to Mike, especially with twelve dogs ready to protect him. I heard the doors to the vehicle open. Were the other humans getting out of the vehicle to cause trouble?

Lakota told me that Mike started to laugh and put his arm around Mister Manhow's shoulders, holding him very tightly. I sensed that Nitro and Brownie went into their alert modes, after I heard Christmas lead the other dogs closer to Mike.

Mike continued to laugh while he said, "So, you are threatening me with an accident if I run this race, and you will have your two friends, over there by your vehicle, do me some damage? I really do not think so." Mike continued, "Actually, I strongly suggest you tell your friends to get back into your vehicle. They would have to deal with four dogs, while I deal with you. As you probably have noticed, I have a very good hold on you and ...."

Mister Manhow quickly understood Mike's message and told the other two humans to stay where they were.

"Do you remember a show called 'Candid Camera'?" Mike asked the men. However, before anyone could answer, Mike said, "Sure you do. Well, Gentlemen, you are on our version of 'Candid Camera'."

Mister Manhow asked, "What do you mean?"

Lakota told me that Mike pointed to the peak of the big house and said, "See that video camera up there? I am sure you do. Well, that camera is on 24/7 and records everything that happens in my dog yard, which we are standing in. We have a lot of wildlife traveling through here, and I like to photograph it. Hey Mister Manhow, do you want to smile for my camera? Aw, come on. Say cheese, please." Mike continued, "Hey you guys over by the car, how about a big smile for my video camera up by the roof of the house." Lakota told me that both humans looked at the camera and then hid behind the vehicle they came in. Not too smart, I thought.

Mike continued, "Do you see that dish next to the camera, Mister

Manhow? Yes, I am sure you do. Well, that is not a satellite dish for TV reception. It is a high-powered, high-tech microphone. I like to record the dogs howling at night at the moon. It is very peaceful and soothing. Maybe you should try it; you do seem a bit stressed. I am sure you would find dog howling very relaxing. Anyway, the microphone is extremely sensitive. It picks up every sound in the yard, including human voices and words such as your threats."

"So, as you can see, Mister Manhow, you have been recorded." Mike continued, "Now, if something does happen to me, I bet the law enforcement folks would welcome the chance to talk to you about any accidents I may have, especially after seeing the video that is being made as we speak."

Lakota told me that Mike let Mister Manhow go and said, "It is time for you to leave my property, Mister Manhow. As I said, I am a very busy man and do not have time for your kind of bad business."

"This is not over Mister Dillingham," Mister Manhow said. "I assure you our paths will cross again."

"I sure hope they do, Mister Manhow, because I really detest unfinished business," Mike continued, "I will assure you, Mister Manhow that the orphanage will be rebuilt, and when our paths do cross again, you have my personal guarantee that I will end this business for good."

Lakota told me that Mister Manhow walked back to his vehicle and left the yard.

Accidents Do Happen

Everybody deserves a day off and so do dogs. We have been training almost every day since Mike decided to run the race to Nome to raise money for rebuilding the orphanage. It feels great to get into our training routine, but a day off prevents burnout, and is good to keep us sharp.

Normally, we start our training runs before the children take off for school. By leaving the kennel early, we do not mess up their routine of getting ready for school. You can bet that we were a bit surprised when the children woke us up calling us "sleepy heads" before the school bus came for them. Yes, a day off!

I felt badly that the children could not stay home and play with us. However, education comes first, play comes next, and what about chow? My tummy reminded me it was chow time, and chow time this morning was late. Normally we would eat and be on the trails before the children gathered at the end of the driveway, waiting for their school bus.

Soon, my thoughts were disrupted by the clanging sound of Mike banging the ladle on the food bucket, and singing (yes, I am being kind calling it that), "Hey you sleepy heads, get your fannies out of bed." Yes, dogs get headaches and we all would get migraines if Mike continued singing. I heard two plops, which meant that Mike dumped two full ladles of chow into my bowl. I felt his hand rubbing my ears as he said, "Chow time Rivey, eat up and enjoy. No trail running today." You have to love this human. While his singing is horrible, he delivers great chow. Yes, I think he is worth keeping!

After we ate and mingled for a while discussing the upcoming race, Lakota told me that Mike came out of the big house to clean up our food bowls and do some kennel chores. Once Mike came into the kennel, he could forget about doing chores. We wanted to play! Brownie and Nitro had the pulling rope. They were trying to wrap it around Mike's legs. Tunny had a few tennis balls, and dropped them at Mike's feet, telling him it was throw and fetch time. Sky and Stormy

raced around the doghouses. Suddenly, they would stop and start play wrestling with each other. Christmas was walking next to Mike, positioning her head under his hand for "mobile ear rubs." There sure was a lot of activity for a day off.

"Okay, Team, work first, then play time," Mike said as Lakota told me Mike picked up the pull rope and tennis balls. "Let me get these chores done and then we will play." All the dogs stopped milling around Mike and he started to do his chores. Lakota told me Mike picked up the food dishes and took them into the warming hut. Lakota and I walked with Mike into the hut. Since Randy and the boys are "camped-out" in the warming hut, Mike moved most of our equipment and sleds to the big shed that Mike calls a garage. However, Mike needed to use the big sink in the warming hut to wash our bowls.

Lakota commented to me that both Mike and Mary keep our food and water bowls very clean. "Come to think of it," he said, "I do not remember ever getting the 'bug' since we started living here. They do a great job of keeping our kennel area clean too."

"You know, you are right, Lakota," I said. "We have it 'made in the shade' here. We have great chow, clean beds, and a nice living area. I guess they know that keeping our area clean keeps us healthy, and a healthy Husky is a happy Husky."

"Sometimes, I have to remind myself that this is not 'Canine Heaven'. We are sure lucky, Rivers," Lakota said. "We sure are."

Lakota told me Mike finished washing the bowls and headed to the yard with the poop scooper. All the humans do poop gathering. Lakota told me that they are very good at it, since there is seldom any in the yard. That is remarkable with the number of dogs who live here.

Once Mike finished washing our bowls, put fresh straw into our doghouses, and scooped the poop, it was playtime. Lakota, Doc, Christmas, and I stood by the gate while the other dogs started gathering around Mike. Lakota told me that Mike grabbed the rope and Nitro charged around the side of one of the doghouses and grabbed the free end on the rope. His idea was to surprise Mike and pull the rope from Mike's hand. However, Mike figured out what Nitro was up to and yanked the rope while Nitro was running with it. Christmas started to laugh as she told me that Nitro stopped cold when Mike yanked the rope.

Christmas told me that Nitro still had the rope in his mouth as he got up from the ground. Nitro was not going to let go of the rope. He

started to pull. So did Mike. This is not the first time these two got into a tug of war. Most of the time, the rope will break. Lakota told me that Mike got a new rope, called "Iron Rope" and it is supposed to be super strong. We will see!

While Nitro is a very big and powerful dog, he must work hard to pull Mike during these games. It was a standoff, neither Mike nor Nitro were budging. Lakota told me that Brownie ran to the rope and grabbed onto it with Nitro. They both pulled and pulled, but they could not budge Mike. He was laughing as they tried to pull him.

Lakota told me that Ugly started his "Ugly Jig" and made Mike laugh. However, soon Ugly grabbed onto the rope and started to pull with his teammates. No matter how hard the three dogs yanked on that rope, Lakota laughed, they could not pull Mike.

Christmas told me that Tunny was talking to Sky and Stormy. Now what were they planning? Christmas told me that Tunny sat very patiently by her tennis balls while her sisters grabbed the rope and started pulling with the other dogs. They could not budge Mike.

I heard the gate open and Mary, with Stryker and Geezer, came into the yard. Nitro asked Stryker and Geezer to join the game. When they did, Christmas told me she saw that mischievous twinkling in Mike's eyes. As soon as the dogs started to yank very hard on the rope, he let it go. We all started to laugh as the dogs tumbled to the ground.

As the dogs were getting up, Mike gave each one of them a big hug and plenty of ear rubs. Nitro sat down and gave Mike his paw. What Nitro told Mike was that Mike won this time, but wait until the next time! That is Nitro for you, he lost honestly, but he will play again, and he believes that next time he may win. Yep, I wonder if that "Iron Rope" would break if Lakota, Christmas, Doc, and I join the other dogs in the "Tug of War" game. Tundra, too, as she also is a very strong Husky.

Barking of Tunny, Christmas told me that as soon as Mike finished giving hugs and ear rubs, she danced around him with a tennis ball in her mouth. Tundra dropped the tennis ball after Mike said, "Drop it." Then Mike picked it up and faked Tunny out by pretending to throw the ball, but really did not. It was still in his hand according to Lakota. Tunny charged off after the ball. However, as soon as she realized Mike never threw it, she raced back and sat in front of Mike, "dancing" all around him while "talking" to him. Mike showed her the ball as he held it in his hand, over his head, teasing Tunny with it. She jumped up; hit Mike by accident and knocked him down. I heard Mike crack his head on a doghouse. Doc said that Mike fell to the ground and did not move.

Lakota told me that all the dogs gathered around Mike and Tundra. Tundra was gently pawing Mike, softly "talking" to him, asking him to get up. Christmas nuzzled Mike's beard.

"Momma, it was an accident," Tunny cried.

"I know, Tunny dear, it is okay," Christmas said to her reassuring her. "Mike will be all right."

"Mike!" It was Mary. Are you okay?"

Doc said there was no blood in the snow by Mike's head. That was a good sign. Christmas said that Mike opened his eyes and he started to get up.

Christmas said Mike looked at Mary and said, "Who are you? Where am I, and why am I sitting here with all of these dogs?"

"Stop kidding me, Mike," Mary said. "I am your wife, these are your dogs, and this is your home."

"I am not kidding. I do not remember you, these dogs, or this place," Mike said.

We heard Mary explain to Mike what had happened. He said he could not remember anything before he woke up on the ground by the doghouse. Mary told Mike she was taking him to the doctor. They left the kennel.

Tunny was still crying as we stood by her. We reassured Tunny it was an accident. She was not listening. She was very angry with herself for hurting her Mike.

Tundra said, "What kind of Husky am I when I hurt my human, my musher? A no-good dog, that is what I am, just a no-good dog." Before any one could say anything, she ran off to her doghouse.

Poor Tunny, it was an accident. I am sure that when Mike comes back, he will understand. We all play as hard as we work. Poor Tunny.

Later that day, Mike came into the yard with Randy. We all knew it was chow time, but there were no banging of the ladle against the food bucket and none of Mike's singing. Randy was telling him about all of the dogs just as Randy would tell a stranger visiting our yard. Mike, a stranger, no way! Nevertheless, it was apparent from the way he was talking to Randy that he did not remember or recognize us.

I did not hear a single dog eat the chow ladled into their bowls. We all waited. From listening to Randy, I knew they were at Tunny's

doghouse. I knew she stayed in there all day after the accident. I heard her crying softly. I heard Randy tell Mike about the accident. Randy was very careful to explain to Mike it was just that, an accident. Tundra is a very sweet dog, a happy-go-lucky dog, and very playful dog. She is very smart, and I am sure you remember, she protected Randy in the last race he ran. She is also very sensitive.

By this time, I felt Stormy come up next to me. She told me all the dogs were watching Mike, Randy, and Tunny.

"Come here, Tundra," Mike said softly. Stormy told me that Tunny poked her head out of her doghouse. Stormy said she still had tears in her eyes.

"Come here, Sweetheart, no one is going to hurt you," Mike said. I heard Tundra come out of her doghouse. Stormy told me Tunny sat in front of Mike. She looked very sorrowful.

Like the rest of us, Tunny has a special bond with Mike, and I bet she feels she broke that bond by knocking Mike down and hurting him. Stormy told me that Mike knelt next to Tundra and gently hugged her.

"Tunny Girl, it is okay. I know you did not mean to hurt me. I know it was an accident and you would never purposely hurt me." Mike continued, "You are still one of my lead dogs Tunny, and I need you to be strong for the race."

Hold on here a minute, we are still racing to Nome, even now after Mike does not remember anything! Now this is good news! We all thought Mike would scrub the race since he cannot remember.

"Now eat your kibble, Tunny, you need to be strong to take me to Nome," Mike said as I heard him stand up. Stormy told me that Tundra looked at Mike, licked his hand, and started to eat her food as Mike told her to do.

Then Mike said to the rest of us, "Eat your chow, you all need to be strong to take me to Nome."

As my nose found my bowl and I started to enjoy the great taste of the food, I overheard Randy and Mike talking.

"Mike, how can you race to Nome?" Randy asked, "you do not remember anything."

Mike replied, "What do I need to remember? Where I have been or where I need to go?" Mike continued, "Do the dogs know the way? Yes. I need to know the basics of caring for them on the trail and driving the team. My instincts and gut feelings will take over.

Since I cannot remember yesterday, I can learn today and be ready for tomorrow's adventure." Mike said, "Besides, my sub-conscious holds all of the memories, skills, knowledge, and experiences. I know they will surface when I need them."

When we finished eating, Mike and Randy collected our food bowls and gave us fresh water. Then they went to the warming hut to wash the bowls. When they returned to the yard, they talked some more about mushing and dogs. We gathered around them for the ear rubs we knew they would give us. Well, that is, all of us except for Tundra. Stormy told me Tunny hung back in her doghouse. I bet she is still angry with herself.

A No-Good Dog

"Uncle Rivers, please wake up."
No matter how deep dogs sleep, we wake up immediately. You bet I
did when I heard the urgency in Christmas' voice.

I asked, "Christmas?"

"I am sorry to wake you, Uncle Rivers, but Tunny is not in her
doghouse," Christmas said. "I went to check on her and she is not
there. You know how upset she was after the accident." Christmas
continued, "Would you walk the yard with me to see if we can find
her?" Christmas told me it was very dark and foggy. She could not
see anything.

"Sure," I said as I climbed out of my doghouse. Once out, I perked
my ears and sniffed the air. I did not smell anything that would tell
me where Tunny would be, but I did hear a scraping sound. I told
Christmas that I heard something. We started to walk in the direction
of the sound I heard.

Since fog can play games with sound, it took me a minute to zero
in on the crying and mumbling, as well as the scraping. I told Christmas to be quiet and walk very slowly. After a few paces, the sounds
became clearer to me.

It was Tunny, crying and repeatedly saying to herself, "I am a no-
good dog. I am a no-good dog."

Christmas asked Tundra, "Tundra, what are you doing?" I noticed
Christmas voice sounded very gentle.

"Momma, I am getting rid of my tennis balls. I do not deserve
them after hurting my Mike today. I am a disgrace to my Husky
heritage. I am a no-good dog." Tunny continued, "Maybe I should
just run away so you would not be embarrassed by what I did. I am
a no-good dog."

I sensed Christmas was barkless with what Tunny said. "That is not
a cool idea Tunny," I said.

"Uncle Rivers! I did not see you standing there in the fog," Tunny

said. "I am an embarrassment to my momma, my sisters, and my uncles. I am just a no-good dog."

"You really think so, Tunny? Well, I do not and neither do your uncles," I said. "You know that running away would cause those who love you more pain than what was caused by the accident." I continued, "You know that beating yourself up over the accident, and calling yourself a 'no-good dog' does not achieve anything whatsoever. It is not only harmful to you, but deeply hurts those who love you."

"Tundra, no matter what you do," Christmas said, "I am your Mother, you are my baby, my daughter, and I will always love you. You are not an embarrassment to me or to anyone else in our family."

I asked Tunny, "Why are you burying your tennis balls?"

She replied, "I do not want them anymore. They are the reason that I hurt my Mike. I do not deserve these toys, these gifts from my Mike. Besides," Tunny continued, "if I do not have them, then there is less chance that I will hurt my Mike in the future."

"Tundra," Christmas asked, "I saw Mike give you a big hug, and I heard him tell you he did not blame you for the accident. Is that correct?"

"Yes, Momma," Tunny replied. "But he does not remember me or you or anybody. He does not even remember himself." Tunny started to sob again.

"Yes, Tunny, he does remember," Christmas said. "Mike's memories, his love for us, and his family are buried deep within him. Nothing will ever take them from him. The door to his memories is just temporarily closed. Mike has not changed, dear Tunny. Believe me, Mike has not changed, and he loves you very much." Christmas continued, "I really do believe that our Mike is still with us, and the door to his memories will open once again."

I chimed in with, "You know, Tunny, we all have accidents. There have been times when our accidents have hurt Mike and his accidents have hurt us."

Tundra asked, "What do you mean, Uncle Rivers?"

"Well," I replied, "How many times has Mike stepped on our paws, by accident? How many times has he accidently clipped us when he cuts our paw nails? Accidents do happen, Tundra. No creature is perfect."

I continued, "How many times do you think I have accidently nipped Mike when he was hand feeding me? Or tripped him when I got underfoot because I could not see him?"

Christmas added, "Uncle Rivers, remember when you and I ran off to save the baby moose. I bet that hurt Mike because he did not know where we were. If I remember, Tunny, you were there also, showing your true Husky heritage by standing with your family protecting a baby who could not protect herself."

"What about that race with Randy? The one Mike could not run because he broke his arm," Christmas said. "First off, you 'talked' Mike into letting Doc run it, and then you warned both Doc and Randy that there was danger near our camp when we took a trail break. You made me very proud."

"What about Mister Bunny?" I asked. "The old sick rabbit that you took in, gave him part of your food, and tried to nurse back to health." I continued, "A lesser dog may have chased that poor old bunny out of the yard. But, not you Tunny, you tried to help him."

"These do not sound like the things a 'no-good dog' would do, Tunny," Christmas said.

"But I hurt my Mike and he lost his memory. He cannot remember who he was, who we are, or what he has done." Tundra said. "I am to blame for that."

Silence. Neither Christmas nor I could convince Tundra that what happened was an accident. She had it set in her mind that she was not a good dog because she betrayed her Husky heritage and hurt her musher. In her mind, she would have to prove she was worthy of Mike's love.

What could I say to make things right? I felt so helpless.

Then I heard a remarkable thing as Christmas said this to her daughter. "Tundra, everything happens for the best. Unfortunately, we may never know what the best is." Christmas paused and then said, "Go to bed, my beautiful young lady dog, and think about what Uncle Rivers and I have said to you." I heard Christmas nuzzle Tunny, and then I heard Tunny walk away to her doghouse.

Silently, Christmas and I returned to our doghouses. I thought about what Christmas, the mother dog, said to her beloved daughter, Tunny. I can only hope that it all makes sense to Tundra. Tunny is too good a dog, too good a Husky, to think she is otherwise.

Take Off

After much preparation, training, and anticipation, we were on Main Street, waiting to start the race. We were pumped up since this race was for the kids, our young friends from the orphanage. However, we were apprehensive. While Mike sounded like Mike, smelled like Mike, and treated us like Mike, he could not remember whom he was. We all wondered if this would affect his ability to guide us to Nome. However, deep down inside, we all knew what Nitro said was true.

"We are taking this man to Nome because he said we need to do that. I do not care if he cannot remember squat. We know he is Mike, and that is all that counts. Enough howling! We have a job to do. We are taking Mike to Nome for those kids. That is why we are in the starting chute today."

The mushing community knew why Mike was running this race. Our buddies on other teams promised to let us know if they sniffed any human danger headed our way. It is good to have friends. Many of the mushers stopping by to wish Mike a safe run. They understood that Mike was not their competition in this race. They knew that our competition was those who wanted to stop us from finishing this race for the kids from the orphanage.

It was getting close to our start time and Randy asked Mike,"What is the dog line up, Mike?"

Mike sounded very relaxed when he replied, "Put Nitro and Brownie in wheel, then Ugly teamed with Fin, and Sky teamed with Stormy. Team Tundra with Doc, and put Christmas with Sunny in the swing dog position. Rivers and Lakota will be the lead dogs." There were only 12 of us racing. Friends offered Mike more dogs to make a 16-dog team. However, he kindly refused, saying that we were his team and all he needed to get this job done.

Randy said, "That is an odd set up, Mike. Normally you have Rivers and Lakota in wheel position."

Mike replied, "Yes, Randy, you are right. We have been training the team with Rivers and Lakota in the wheel position. However, this probably is their last race, and I bet Rivers or Lakota have never lead their team out of the starting chute." Mike continued, "Besides, we have people watching us that want us to fail. I want them to get the message that we do not fear them. They can try to stop us, they will not succeed."

Wow, Lakota and I are the lead dogs starting this race! What a surprise. Mike is right; Lakota and I have never started any race in the lead position. This will be so cool.

Lakota told me he was thrilled to be one of the starting lead dogs on what may be our last race together. I asked him if he heard what Mike said about the people watching us. He told me he did and he knows Mike is right. If we let the bad guys make us fearful, then we lose.

As we talked, Lakota told me that a woman was walking towards Mike. The lady wore a jacket with the letters "KDOGS TV Channel 47" on it.

"Hi, Mister Dillingham," the woman said.

Mike answered, "Please call me Mike, unless you want to sell me something."

The woman laughed. "No, I would like to interview you before the race begins. Is that okay with you?"

"Sure," Mike replied.

"We are going live, ready? Good morning, this is Megan Carver from KDOGS TV 47 live here at the start of the 'Big Race to Nome'. I am standing with Mike Dillingham, who is getting ready to take off on his adventure to Nome." Megan continued,"Mike, is it true that you are running this race to earn money to rebuild the orphanage destroyed by the recent earthquake, and make it free and clear of debt?"

Mike: "Yes. We have received 'Paw Pledges' from people, children, schools, and industry, pledging money for each mile we complete. The further we go, the more money is donated. There are a few donors who will double their contribution if we complete the race. We need about $500,000. Right now we have about $275,000 pledged."

Megan: "Amazing. I notice that you are running Rivers in lead. I understand he is blind. Is that correct?"

Mike: "Yes. Rivers has been blind for a long time. While a seasoned racer and veteran of this race, Rivers has never lead his team out of the starting chute. Since this will probably be his last race, and may be the only time we will race together, I feel he should be one of my lead dogs today."

85

Megan: "You have that much confidence in Rivers?"

Mike: "Yes. Rivers has never failed me. He can do this. I know he wants to do it, he will do it, and he has the courage to succeed. We are a team and today, he is one of my lead dogs."

Megan: "I understand your other lead dog, Lakota, recently had a kidney removed due to cancer. Is he fit to race and be a lead dog"?

Mike: "Yes. The vets cleared Lakota for this race. Lakota and Rivers work as a team. They have worked very hard for me since coming to live with me several years ago. They deserve to lead this team on what may be their final race. Besides, Lakota made the decision to run this race. He would not allow me to leave him home. He knows he will cross the finish line in Nome, even if I have to carry him on my shoulders."

Megan: "To change the subject, word on the street is that you have been threatened because you want to save the orphanage from some land developers. Is that true?"

Mike: "Word on the street, Megan? News to me. Just let me say that I had a visitor whose words I understood to be a subtle threat. His words or the threat, if real, will not stop the dogs or I from finishing this race and rebuilding the orphanage."

Megan: "One last question. I understand you had an accident a few months ago and lost your memory. Are you suffering from amnesia?"

Mike, chuckling: "Yes, that is true. Well, I am an old geezer and forgetful anyway. Therefore, I do not consider that a problem. I need to get going, Megan. My wife Mary or Randy or Caitlyn can answer any other questions you have. Thank you. I appreciate your time with this."

Megan: "No, Mike, thank you for giving me a truly remarkable story. Good luck to you and your team in your race to Nome."

As Mike rejoined the team, I heard Megan say, "The race to Nome is a trail of many stories. Here we have a musher who has no memory; racing his team, led by his blind dog, to Nome, for the sole purpose of earning money to rebuild our local orphanage. The threats to prevent this team's victory add some edginess to this story. You can be sure I will keep you up-to-date on this story. By the way, KDOGS donated $1000 to the orphanage rebuilding project and challenges all other Alaska media outlets to do the same."

"It is time to move the team, Randy," Mike said. "You drive the sled and I will walk the lead dogs."

"Okay, Mike. Team, walk," Randy commanded. Mike had a leash

on me to guide me down Main Street as we waited our turn to start the race. When Randy commanded, "Walk," we knew that we were to walk, not run, or jump. Yes, we were very excited, but we wanted to make Mike proud of how well behaved we were. Besides, there was no point in wasting energy now that we might need later on the trail.

"Team, stop. Team, sit," Randy commanded as he mushed us down Main Street. We stopped and sat. We would continue this routine until it was our turn in the starting chute.

I knew there was a huge crowd watching us. I heard the announcer say, "Next is Mike Dillingham with his Green and Gold team led by his blind dog, Rivers and Lakota, a cancer survivor. As you may know, Mike's team is racing to Nome to raise money to rebuild the Quiet Tundra Orphanage. The recent earthquake destroyed the orphanage. By the way, our station KMUSH TV meets the $1000 challenge of KDOGS. If any of our listeners want to make a donation, please come to the announcer's booth."

"Wow, we sure are getting a lot of attention," I had to bark at Lakota because the cheering was so loud.

"Yes," Lakota barked. "The more attention we receive, the more money we get for the kids." Lakota continued, "We do look sharp as a team with our green and gold harnesses and lines. The sled bag looks as if it was just washed, and Mike has his green and gold snowsuit on. I even saw green and gold dog coats in the sled bag. Yes, we do look good."

"2 minutes," was the timekeeper's call. Lakota told me that Mike was walking to the front of the team. I heard him kneel in front of me. Mike told me as he rubbed my ears, "Enjoy this run, Rivers, you deserved the lead dog slot. Show them what you can do. Lead us out of town and on to the trail to Nome." He gave me a hug and then moved over to Lakota.

I heard him whisper to Lakota, "I am not leaving you on the trail if you get sick and cannot go on. I will carry you to Nome. You deserve to finish this race and you will, my buddy."

Lakota told me that Mike moved to each dog giving each dog some ear rubs and some words of love and encouragement. Christmas, who was just behind me said," Oh Uncle Rivers, I saw fiery demons in Mike's eyes and not the mischievous Santa Claus twinkle that used to be there. I hope Santa returns, the demons scare me."

Lakota heard Christmas and said to her, "I have seen those demons before in other humans who were driven. They will let nothing stop them from achieving their goal. I believe Mike's demons are our friends on this trail run. Do not be afraid of them, 'Little One'. Once we return home from Nome, I know the demons will vanish."

"I hope so," Christmas said. I heard her turn to her babies, Tundra, Stormy, and Sky, and ask, "Are you ready to show this crowd what grown up lady dogs you are?"

"Yes, Momma we are going to make you and Mike very proud of us," Sky barked.

"You betcha," barked Stormy.

Then Tundra answered her Mom with a very low voice, almost like a growl, "Let's rock!" Wow, Tunny sounded very serious.

"Tunny Girl," Mike said. Lakota told me Mike was giving Tundra a big hug. "Have some fun with this race, Tundra, I am okay." Lakota told me that Tundra gave Mike a big kiss on his nose. That was so cool. Tundra has been moping around since the accident. Now, maybe she can get back to being a happy dog.

"30 seconds," said the timekeeper. Lakota told me Mike was on the runners. He kissed Mary, then Caitlyn and gave a big hug to Randy.

"15 seconds." Lakota told me that Mike put on his gloves. There was a big smile on his face.

"10 seconds."

"5." I heard Mike pull the snow hook.

"4." "Team, stand tall!" Mike commanded.

"3." "Look sharp."

"2." "Get ready."

"1." "Take Off! Hike! Hike!"

I leaned into my harness and felt the gang line grow tight as twelve determined dogs jumped off the starting line and headed down Main Street. The crowd was cheering us on. I heard one group of voices that I recognized. It was Mrs. Astor and the children from the orphanage chanting, "Go, team, go! Go, team, go!" However, one voice stood out. A young boy's voice I recognized from the orphanage, "Tunny, you go girl!" So Tundra has a fan, I hope she heard him. She must have because I heard her howl just for him.

We were on our way, to meet our destiny.

Changes In The Night

Lakota and I lead the team out-of-town, past the crowds, and into the wilderness. We ran at a nice even pace. Surprisingly, no other teams passed us. However, we did pass a few teams resting on the side of the road. According to Lakota, we seemed to be holding our own. That was not bad for a team of retired racing sled dogs, lead by a blind dog and a cancer survivor.

So far, this run was a nice trail run; but I knew, as we headed further into the wilderness, things would become challenging and maybe even dangerous.

"Gee. Gee," were Mike's commands to Lakota and me to lead the team off the trail. "Whoa, Team," was Mike's command for us to stop. "Break time," he said. I know Mike has a running/break-time schedule that he will try to keep us on. We run for while, and then we rest for an equal amount of time. During our runs on the trail, Mike will stop us for short snack breaks. After a short, snack break, Mike may replace the lead dogs with fresh dogs from other team positions. He does this so that each lead dog will get a break from leading. Leading a team can be very stressful and tiring. By chang-ing leaders often, Mike will always have fresh leaders. Having fresh leaders is a good thing, especially if the trail gets bad, the weather becomes nasty, or if we meet the unexpected and dangerous. Since the weather and trail were nice, I bet Mike will put two of the younger dogs in the lead position, and move Lakota and me back to our normal wheel positions.

I cannot tell you how surprised I was when Mike did not change leaders after this snack break. Lakota and I were still in our lead dog position as Mike gave us the command to stand tall and start back down the trail.

Lakota told me it was getting dark. The darkness is not a problem for me, but it can be for the rest of the team. "Rivers," Lakota asked, "I wonder why Mike did not change leaders when we took that last break."

"I am not sure, Lakota," I replied. "Maybe he has a different plan

for running this race." Yes, it was strange for Mike not to change the lead dogs.

A short while later Mike gave the "Gee, Gee" command. This command would take us off the trail. Lakota told me that there was a trail to our right and Mike wanted us to take it. Why would Mike want to get off the main trail?

Lakota told me that the side trail went into a grove of trees. Once we were into the grove, Mike gave us the "Stop" command and then the "Sit" command.

As we sat, I heard Mike plant the snow hook and move down the team giving us plenty of praise and ear rubs. After that, he snacked us again. Hmm, no hot chow, I thought. That can only mean that we are going back on the trail, and this will only be a short break. This is very different from our normal run schedule.

I heard something and asked, "What is that sound?"

Nitro replied, "I hear it also." Then Nitro said, "The sound is coming from Mike. There is a buzzing thing on his face. The thing is eating Mike's beard. The beard is gone!"

I heard Nitro start to growl and sound like he was going to attack the thing that ate Mike's beard.

"Easy, Nitro," Mike said. "It is okay. I just shaved my beard off." I thought I heard Mike chuckle when I said that. Funny, none of us knows what Mike looks like without his beard. I hope Lakota or Stormy tell me. I am curious. What does Mike look like without his face fur?

Next, I heard Mike unzip the sled bag. Brownie told me Mike took out all of our equipment, including another sled bag. It was the old sled bag. The one we used a long time ago. The old sled bag is a plain black one. Brownie told us that Mike replaced our green and gold sled bag with the black sled bag, by attaching the black bag to our sled. Then, Brownie told us Mike reloaded all of our equipment into the black bag. Changing out sled bags made me wonder, why would Mike do that?

I heard Mike walk to me. He unhooked my tug and necklines and removed my harness. Stormy told me Mike changed my harnesses to a black one. Stormy said that Mike changed all the dogs' harnesses to black ones. Lakota told me Mike also changed the gangline, neckline, and tug lines to black ones. Mike then stowed our green and gold lines, our green and gold harnesses, and the green and gold sled bag

into the black sled bag. You can believe me; we were all wondering what was going on. Why was Mike hiding our team colors?

After stowing our green and gold gear, Mike moved us into our new team positions. Mike put Christmas and Sky in lead and moved Lakota and me back to our normal wheel position. Mike told us that we did a great job as his lead dogs, leading the team past the crowds, into the wilderness, and down the trail. I heard another zipper unzip and asked Lakota what Mike was doing now.

Lakota said that Mike took off his green parka and snowsuit. He then changed into a plain black one. Lakota said it looked old and worn. Ugly said that the harnesses and lines look old and worn also. "We look like a ragtag bunch of dogs rather than the sharp team that left the starting chute," Ugly said. He did not sound like a happy camper. Ugly takes pride in his appearance.

I guess Mike noticed the confusion in our faces because he said, "The bad guys, who are chasing us, will be looking for a sharp looking team, a team with green and gold colors and a musher with a beard. They will not be looking for a team in black colors and a musher with no beard. I hope that we will blend into the pack of mushers running the race. By running with the pack, we should go unnoticed. For a short while, the green and gold team will disappear. I promise you, we will change back into our green and gold colors once we get closer to Nome.

"Now, it all makes sense," Doc said. "This is a great plan, guys. The bad guys will not be able to find us because they are looking for a team with our team colors. Those team colors just disappeared. All we need to do is run with the pack all the way to Nome."

The plan worked very well. We were having a great run. That is, until a bad snowstorm hit the trail and caused the pack to spread out. After that, we were on our own.

On The Trail

The gentle sound of the sled runners gliding on the snow came to a sudden end. I heard the snow machine come up behind us before any of my teammates did. I started to bark and turned my head towards Mike.

"Rivers, what is it?" Mike asked. However, I guess he heard the "Iron Dog" because he said, "They have found us Team. Now the fun begins."

I was waiting for Mike to unzip the sled bag and take out his rifle. His rifle would be the only protection we would have against the "Iron Dog." If the snow machine ran into the team, well, it sure would be messy.

As I heard the "Iron Dog" closing in, Lakota told me that Mike already had his rifle out and slung over his shoulder. Mike told Christmas and Sunny, the lead dogs, "Girls keep it steady. Do not be afraid. I will take care of the 'Iron Dog'."

Stormy must have looked back because she told me Mike turned around on the runners and so that he could point his rifle at the 'Iron Dog'."

"Bam! Bam! Bam!" I heard three shots that sounded very loud. Lakota told me that Mike is not using his regular rifle, but a new shinny one. I bet it must be very powerful to sound that loud. I heard the "Iron Dog" stop. Lakota told me the snow machine stopped so quickly that the driver flew over the front of it and almost fell into our team!

"Christmas, Whoa. Sunny, Whoa," Mike commanded the team to stop. Then Mike said, "Team, sit." As we sat, I heard Mike plant the snow hook. Lakota told me Mike took Nitro and Brownie off the gang line and said, "Nitro, Brownie, come with me, we have some work to do".

Lakota said that Mike took some rope out of the sled bag and walked over to where the driver was laying in the snow. Lakota told me that Mike grabbed the driver by the collar of his snowsuit, and dragged him to the "Iron Dog," which, according to Lakota, was very

smashed up. Mike tied the driver to the snow machine. Mike then removed the driver's helmet.

Mike told Nitro and Brownie to stay by the driver. "If he moves, bark, boys," Mike said as I heard him walk back towards the team.

I heard Nitro tell Brownie, "I really do not like this human. He tried to hurt our Mike and the team. Do you think Mike would get angry with me if I shake this human up a bit?"

Brownie replied, "Now Nitro, be nice. Our job is to finish this race for the kids from the orphanage, while protecting Mike and the rest of the team. I am sure Mike has plans for this human. Besides, Stryker told me these bad humans taste terrible. Might make you sick and you do not want that."

"Good point," Nitro replied. "Hmm, the human is starting to move." I heard Nitro and Brownie both start to bark and growl at the driver.

Lakota told me that the driver's eyes opened up and he was startled when he saw Nitro and Brownie barking right into his face.

I heard Mike command, "Stop Nitro, Stop Brownie," as he walked over to the driver. Mike said, "So, you woke up, Sleeping Beauty; good, we need to have a little chat."

"I have nothing to say to you," the driver said.

"Are you sure about that?" Mike continued, "I think you would want to tell me about yourself, and who sent you out here to get me. And course, I would like to know how many more snow machiners are looking for me."

Silence, the driver was not talking.

"Hmm, I guess you are the strong silent type. Maybe I will just shoot you and leave you here for the wildlife to feed on. I really have no time to deal with you."

The driver said, "You would not do that. If you wanted to shoot me, you could have when you shot at my snow machine and made it stop." I could sense the fear in the driver's voice.

"True, I should have and could have, but I wanted to talk to you. Do not count your blessings just yet, friend. Keep in mind that if you do not start talking very soon, then I have no use for you. I have little mercy for those that want to hurt my dogs," Mike said. "I know your job was to stop me and my team from finishing this race any way you could. So, what is good for the goose is good for the gander, right?" Mike continued, "No matter what you do now, you lose. So, make it easy on yourself and start talking."

Silence, the driver said nothing.

"Which one are you, stubborn or stupid?" Mike asked. "It makes no difference to me. It is getting dark. The temperatures are dropping and you will be here all by yourself when we leave. This is wolf and bear country. As soon as the team and I move down the trail, the wolves will come to see if we left any food behind. They will smell you and consider you a free meal, fast food actually." Mike chuckled. "Have you ever seen a wolf up close?" Mike asked. Lakota told me the driver shook his head no. "I thought so. Let me give you an idea what is in store for you once we move on." Lakota told me that Mike turned to Nitro, who was sitting very patiently by Mike's side.

"Nitro, you want to give this Gentleman a preview of what the wolves will do when they get here?" On cue, Nitro growled, sneered, and snapped right in front of the driver's face. "Good boy, Nitro, that is enough. We do not want to scare the poor man too much."

The driver timidly asked, "If I talk, will you get me out of here?"

"I make no promises until I hear what you have to say," Mike replied.

The driver started to tell Mike everything. He told Mike there was only one other "Iron Dog" on the trail. That was a lie. I heard the sounds of two additional and different *Iron Dogs*!

"Thanks," Mike said, "I have it all on tape. I know a friend of mine with the State Troopers who will enjoy your story, especially the part about Mister Manhow hiring you to stop us."

The driver said, "Okay, I told you wanted you wanted to know. What happens to me now? You are not going to leave me here for the wolves, are you?"

"Well, yes, I am," Mike said. "We are about a two hour run from the end of this race. Once I finish the race, I will send the State Troopers out for you. There are several mushers behind me so you will not be totally alone for the two hours it takes me to get to the finish line." Mike continued, "Your snow machine will not run, not after what I did to it. Therefore, you are stuck here. By the way, there are no wolves in the area. The bears are hibernating and will not wake up for a few more weeks. There are moose, but they are not meat eaters."

Lakota told me that Mike moved the broken snow machine and the driver off the trail. As he did, I heard the second "Iron Dog." I started barking. "Okay Rivers, I hear it." Mike said as I heard him run towards the sled. Nitro and Brownie were right with him.

Lakota told me that we were off the trail, separate from the main trail by some small trees. The trees will prevent the snow machine from getting to us. I heard Mike unzip the sled bag. Lakota told me Mike took out our second snow hook with the long rope attached to it. Mike took all of the dogs off the gang line, and told the team, "You are free to run away if I cannot stop this 'Iron Dog'. Run the trail to the finish line. Randy is there waiting for you." Mike continued, "Stormy, you stay with Lakota and Rivers and make sure they get home. Doc, Brownie, Ugly and Nitro, you know this trail, as well as Rivers and Lakota. Please make sure the young dogs get home. Now go!"

Lakota told me that Mike slipped between the trees and into the darkness of the night.

"Gang, there are two 'Iron Dogs' out there, not just the one Mike heard. He will be ambushed."

Tundra said she could see the trail between the trees and a light coming down the trail towards Mike. "Yes," Christmas said, "The light is getting brighter and brighter as it comes down the trail. It is the second 'Iron Dog'."

Ugly asked, "Where is Mike?"

"Look," Doc said, "he is standing in the middle of the trail. You can faintly see him in the 'Iron Dog's' head light."

Sky asked, "Why is Mike standing in the middle of the trail? The 'Iron Dog' will run over him."

"Look," Brownie said. "Mike is twirling the snow hook in a big circle over his head."

"I wonder what he is planning to do," Nitro said.

"I bet he is going to use the snow hook to knock the driver off the 'Iron Dog'," Tunny said. "Randy read stories to us about people who use bolos as weapons."

"Bolos?" Ugly said.

Stormy answered, "Yes, Uncle Ugly. Bolos are three rocks tied together and then tied to a long rope so that a human can twirl it over his head. When the human lets it go, aimed at the target, the three rocks wrap around the target. Randy showed us pictures of bolos in the books he read to us." Stormy added, "They look very simple but appear to be very dangerous."

Tunny said, "That snow hook is very heavy. Once Mike gets it up to the speed he wants and aims it, he will let it go at the driver of the 'Iron Dog'. If it hits the driver, it will knock him off the snow machine."

Sky added, "The problem is that Mike must let the 'Iron Dog' get close to him before he can throw the snow hook. Once he lets it go, Mike needs to jump out of the way of the snow machine."

Stormy said, "The snow machine could hit Mike once the driver is knocked off."

Sunny asked, "Could Mike shoot the 'Iron Dog' like he did to the other one?"

"No, Sunny, this 'Iron Dog' is too far away and Mike might hit the driver," Lakota said. "I do not think Mike wants to do that. By knocking the driver off the 'Iron Dog', Mike can tie him up like he did the first driver, and let the State Troopers deal with them."

Christmas barked, "Look! The 'Iron Dog' is almost on top of Mike." She told us that Mike let the snow hook go and then jumped into a snow bank by the tree line. The snow hook smashed through the windscreen of the "Iron Dog" and hit the driver, knocking him off the snow machine. We all cheered. But wait, I heard the third "Iron Dog".

"Gang, I hear the third 'Iron Dog', we must warn Mike." Stormy told me that Mike was in the middle of the trail dealing with the driver of the second "Iron Dog". His back was to the third snow machine.

"I do not think Mike can hear the 'Iron Dog' coming at him," Lakota said.

"I must stop that 'Iron Dog' from hitting my Mike," Tunny barked as she fearlessly took off in the direction of the third "Iron Dog".

"No!" Christmas barked. However, Lakota told me it was too late. Tundra was already chasing down the third "Iron Dog" . Lakota told me that Tundra caught up to the "Iron Dog" and leaped at the driver. As Tunny grabbed the driver by his arm, I heard him scream in pain. They both fell off the "Iron Dog", tumbling over each other on the ground. Tunny was not moving. The driver started to get up.

"Tunny!" Christmas howled and she raced off to deal with the driver. Sky followed.

"Uncle Rivers, I have to go and take care of my sister," Stormy said as she raced off to join her sisters and Mother. Lakota told me the driver got up and was about to kick Tunny, but Christmas and Sky both jumped at him, knocked him down, and pinned him to the ground. I heard Christmas bark and growl at the driver. She was in full rage. If that driver makes a move, well, who knows what Christmas will do. Lakota also said that Tunny was still not moving. Stormy sat down by her twin sister, Tunny.

Nitro said, "Fin, Lakota, Rivers, and Sunny, you go and help Christmas. Make sure that driver does not get up. Ugly, Doc, Brownie, and I will go help Mike.

We ran to where Nitro told us to go. Lakota led me to Tunny. "Rivers," Lakota said. "Fin, Sunny, and I are going to help Christmas with the driver. Will you be okay if I left you by Tunny and Stormy?"

"Yes," I replied, "Christmas needs to be with her baby, Tunny. You take care of that driver until Mike gets there."

I heard Lakota tell Christmas to go to Tunny, and that he, Fin and Sunny would pin the "Iron Dog" driver until Mike can deal with him up. Christmas answered Lakota with a voice I never heard her use before. "Yes, Uncle Lakota, but if my baby is seriously hurt, this dude will learn first paw what it is like to deal with a one very upset momma dog!" I heard Christmas and Sky's paw steps race to where Tunny, Stormy, and I were.

Before Christmas and Sky returned, I sniffed Tunny. I could hear her breathing.

"Aunt Sandy, will Tunny be okay?" Stormy asked. Sandy was here, I thought. Then I saw her. This was Sandy's gift to me. I can see while she visits us.

I heard Christmas race to where Tunny was resting. "My poor Tunny, what have you done to yourself?

I heard Aunt Sandy say, "Tunny will be fine. She is just a bit dazed from falling with the driver."

Christmas replied, "Tundra still blames herself for causing Mike to lose his memory. I do not know how to help Tunny to stop blaming herself for the accident and feeling so badly. We all know it was an accident."

"Little One," Sandy said, using Christmas' old nickname, "Mike will take care of that for you." Sandy continued, "Christmas, you have done a great job raising your babies. They are fine Huskies and true champions. You make me very proud."

Then Sandy turned to me and said, "Rivers, you and the team have done a great job getting Mike through this race and helping those poor children from the orphanage. I know you, as well as the rest of the team, are very concerned about Mike and his memory. Well, I can tell you that Mike is not what he appears to be, and you will find out very shortly that things are okay."

Sandy nuzzled Christmas, Sky, and Stormy. Then I saw her sit by Tunny. Sandy put her paw on Tunny's shoulder, bent over, and nuzzled

Tunny's ear. I saw Tunny's eyes open as she jumped up. "Aunt Sandy!" Tunny said. "What are you doing here?"

"Why, I am looking after one of my babies on this trail, Tundra. You did a very brave thing saving Mike like that. I just want you to know he is okay and you need not blame yourself for knocking him down in the kennel." She continued, "I must go, Mike is coming, and he must get you back in team formation and on the trail to finish this race. Those children need you. So finish this race for them."

She nuzzled Tunny again and was gone. My darkness returned.

Onward To The Finish

After Mike moved the third "Iron Dog" off the trail and tied the driver to it, he came back to where we were. "Great job, Team, I am really proud of you." Stormy then told me that Mike knelt next to Tunny and said, "That was a very brave thing you did, Tunny Girl, knocking that driver off the snow machine and protecting me. Thank you." With that, Stormy told me Mike gave Tunny a very long body hug. I heard Mike gently whispering to Tundra what a good dog she was.

"Okay Team, it is time to finish this race in our green and gold team colors!" Mike told us to go back to the sled. Lakota told me that Mike took our green and gold gear out of the sled bag. He put our harnesses on us and hooked our lines up to the sled. He then took everything out of the sled bag, including our green and gold sled bag and changed the bags. After he reloaded the equipment, Mike put on his green and gold snowsuit and parka. Then Mike put his racing bib on with our team number on it. "We are ready to finish this race," he said. "If there are any more bad guys out there, they are going to have to chase us to Nome!"

When he hooked us up to the gang line, Mike put Tunny and Doc in the lead dog positions. Stormy was with Sky in the swing dog position, Sunny and Christmas were together as was Ugly with Fin. Mike put Nitro and Brownie together. Lakota and I were in the wheel position. Once we were ready, Mike gave us the command, "Hike!", and we started to race down the trail.

Tundra was doing a great job as a lead dog. She maintained a very nice pace and kept the gang line straight, with no slack in it. I know Tunny was making her mom very proud as she perfectly completed every command Mike gave the leaders.

As we raced down the trail, I became lost in my thoughts of this adventure. I was letting my mind's eye recall all of the things that happened since the earthquake. However, Lakota's words bought me out of my thoughts. "Rivers, I cannot make it."

I guess Mike must have seen that Lakota was having difficulty keeping up with us. I heard, "Tundra, Whoa. Doc, Whoa." Mike commanded the team to stop. We did. "Team, sit." We sat. I heard Mike plant the snow hook and step off the runners. I heard him kneel by Lakota. "Okay, Lakota buddy, time for your ride in the basket. You have done a great job. You deserve to ride the rest of the way to the finish line."

I heard Mike unsnap Lakota's neck and tug lines from the gangline. "Come on, Lakota, time go to the basket," Mike gently said to him.

"I am not going to ride in the basket," Lakota said. "I am a Husky, and I will finish this race in my position for my musher."

"Lakota," I said. "You are letting your foolish pride blind you and you are being stubborn. You are the oldest dog on this team. You have only one kidney. You have an ongoing battle with cancer. You ran a great race. You protected your musher. You have been a very faithful dog to Mike." I continued, "If you are stubborn and insist on running some more, you could be a dead dog, and that would hurt Mike. Think about it."

Lakota is a thinker. It took him only a heartbeat to decide. "Rivers, you are right," Lakota said. "Sometimes I do get stubborn. Thanks." I heard him get up and walk with Mike to the sled basket.

I heard Mike say to Lakota, "Good boy. You did a great job, Lakota, I am very proud of you." Nitro told me Mike gave Lakota a big hug as he helped him into the sled basket.

Mike moved Nitro into Lakota's wheel position and put Brownie in front of me as my team guide dog.

"Lakota," It was Nitro. "I am very proud to be your friend and teammate; we could not have raced this adventure without you." Nitro continued, "As Mike promised, you will finish this race with us."

I heard all my teammates bark similar good things to Lakota. He knew they were all very sincere about their feelings towards him. I am sure the team's positive comments made Lakota feel very good and know he did not disgrace his Husky heritage because he could not finish the race in his team position.

We started back down the trail. Lakota kept telling me what was around me, just as he did when he runs next to me.

After another brief stop at a building along the trail, we reached Nome and crossed the finish line. Mike gave us the stop and sit commands. Doc told us to sit tall and be proud. We did it! We finished the race for the children from the orphanage. This race was an interesting adventure. I am just glad this one is over. It is one thing running a race. It sure becomes a different race when bad dudes are chasing you.

There is an end of race equipment check done by the race officials. The check is actually the final qualifier for completing the race. If we do not pass the equipment check, then we officially did not finish the race.

The race officials asked Mike why Lakota was in the basket. Mike told them Lakota was okay. Mike just wanted to give his old buddy a break. I heard Lakota jump out of the sled basket so the race officials could check the equipment in the sled bag.

Since there were no people around the finish line, I can only assume it was very late at night or early morning. Lakota told me that he was standing by Mike's side, watching the team, as the officials checked our equipment.

Something was just not right; I heard footsteps running at us.

"Lakota," I said. "Look to your right, what do you see?"

"There is a human running at us with a big stick in his hands. He is screaming at Mike. He is going to hit Mike!"

Nitro told me that just before the human could strike Mike, Lakota jumped at the man, hitting the man in the chest. As the man started to fall to the ground, he hit Lakota with the big stick. Lakota went down. The team got excited and started to move towards Mike and the human falling to ground.

"Team, sit, now!" Mike commanded. We sat, but we were not too happy that someone tried to hurt our Mike and Lakota. Meanwhile, Stormy told me that Mike turned around just in time to grab the stick from the human's hand as the human fell to ground. The human screamed that Mike broke his wrist.

Nitro told me that Mike threw the stick towards the sled and said, "Mister, if I were you, I would stay down on the ground. Do not get up." The tone in Mike's voice was very threatening. Nitro told me there was great fear and pain in the man's face. He did not get up. Nitro started that low menacing growl of his, indicating he is going into full rage. I think he got the human's attention. I know Nitro got mine. I was starting to worry that Nitro might become uncontrollable.

Stormy told me that the race officials stopped checking the equipment. One of them said to Mike. "Mike, go tend to your dog, we will watch this guy. I will call the State Troopers."

"Thanks," I heard Mike say as I heard him kneel by Lakota.

"Lakota," I asked, "are you okay."

"I think so. Just dazed, the stick hit me in the rear hip. Is Mike okay?"

"Yes, Mike is fine, Lakota," Ugly said. "Mike did a real number on that human when he grabbed the big stick after you jumped the dude."

Doc added, "The dude will not be writing any love letters for a while with that hand. I thought I heard it snap when Mike took the big stick away from him."

Brownie added. "Wow Lakota, you hit that dude almost at head level. He swung the stick at you, hitting your hip as he was going down. I did not think an old dog like you could jump so high. Man, that guy hit the ground very hard. Nice hit, Lakota."

"Uncle Lakota," Christmas said. "Just lay still until Mike checks you out."

"I am fine, 'Little One'," Lakota answered Christmas.

I heard another set of footsteps come towards us. "Hi Mike, how is my Sunny? Why is Lakota down? What is going on here? You need help Mike?" It was Doctor Jim. I bet he flew up here to get his Sunny after the race was over.

"Hi, Doctor Jim," Mike answered. "Lakota finished the race in the basket. He was a bit tired and I did not want to stress him. He was standing next to me as the officials checked our gear. The man on the ground over there tried to attack me with a baseball bat. Lakota must have heard the man running at us because Lakota jumped the man before the jerk could clobber me. Unfortunately, Lakota got hit and went down."

"Hey you! Are you a doctor? I demand you look at my wrist, now! That bozo standing next to you broke it," The human on the ground screamed at Doctor Jim. This human was becoming annoying.

"Shut up, mister, or else I will let Mike feed you to his dogs. They look like they want a piece of you." Way to go race official, I thought. The man kept quite after that. He must have taken a good look at eleven dogs staring at him, especially Nitro, who continued his low menacing growl.

As Doctor Jim went to Lakota's side, he calmly said to the man on the ground, "I am a veterinarian, not a medical doctor, and not licensed to provide you with medical care. Besides, your injuries do not appear to be life threatening. Hitting a dog with a baseball bat can cause serious injuries."

Stormy told me that Doctor Jim looked at Lakota, gently touching Lakota's hip. Doctor Jim then asked Lakota to sit up. Lakota stood up and shook as if he were shaking water from his coat. He then sat down and raised his paw for Doctor Jim to shake. I heard Mike chuckle.

"Mike, I think Lakota is okay, probably just stunned and sore. I am sure his hip is bruised, but I do not think anything is broken," Doctor Jim said. "He is a tough old dog. To be on the safe side, I would like to take Lakota to the local vet clinic and do some X-rays."

Mike replied, "Sounds good to me. I will catch up to you later and pick up Lakota."

Stormy told me Mike walked over to the sled bag, got out a leash, the first aid kit, and a broken trail marker. He then walked back to where Doctor Jim and Lakota were. I heard Mike clip the leash on Lakota's collar, and say to him, "You go with Doctor Jim, Lakota. Let him check your hip. I will come and get you when I am finished here. Thanks buddy, for stopping that man from hurting me." Stormy told me that Mike put a big hug on Lakota, and Lakota licked Mike's nose.

As Doctor Jim and Lakota walked off to the vet clinic, Stormy told me Mike walked to where the human was laying on the ground. Now remember, I am next to Nitro and he has not said too much. Stormy told me Nitro just sat there, staring at the human on the ground. Brownie told me he recognized the human as the one who visited our kennel and threatened Mike about running the race. I thought I recognized that voice.

I was getting a bit worried about Nitro. He continued growling with that low menacing tone of his. He was giving the human on the ground fair warning. "Make a move on Mike and you will answer to me." I knew there was only one thing preventing Nitro from going after the human on the ground, Mike's command to sit. If that human tries to hurt Mike, Nitro will move this entire team and sled to get to him. Huskies protect their musher, just as Lakota saved Mike. If Nitro goes into full rage, Mike will have his hands full and so will the human on the ground.

"Let me see your wrist," Mike demanded.

"Why? Are you going to hurt me some more?" The man asked.

"No, I am going to splint your wrist," Mike replied. "If I was going to hurt you, I would have done it after you hit my dog with that baseball bat." Mike continued, "Consider yourself lucky you are dealing with me instead of that big dog on my team who is staring you down.

I am sure you can hear him growling at you. If you had hit me, he, and probably every dog on the team would have ... well you really do not want to know. Nitro is that dog's name. He is very powerful and capable of moving the entire team and equipment to run you down. He would not stop until he does. As I said, consider yourself lucky. Be smart and do not move while I tend to your wrist."

"You ruined me," the man said after I heard Mike break the trailer marker. Stormy told me that Mike broke it into two pieces. He then placed one piece on each side of the wrist and started to wrap it with a bandage from the first aid kit.

"Ruined you, Mister Manhow?" Mike said. "I only broke your wrist and I am not sure if it is really broken."

"No, you ruined me financially. I had all of my money tied up in building a new development where the orphanage stood." The man continued, "Since you finished this race, I lost everything."

Mike replied, "If that is true, Mister Manhow, then you actually lost everything before this race even started."

"What do you mean?" Mister Manhow snarled.

Mike replied, "After the earthquake, Mrs. Astor, who runs and owns the orphanage, told me about a land developer who had her bank put pressure on her regarding her loan. One of the vice presidents of that bank is a good friend of mine and a supporter of the orphanage. With Mrs. Astor's approval, I paid off the existing loan. The title, land, and mineral rights belong to a foundation I started to protect the orphanage and provide for its future."

Mike said, "The lowlife you paid at the bank to do your dirty work, a Mister Vandergoat, was fired and may go to jail, once this race is over. The bank does not tolerate treating their long term customers badly." Mike added, "My friend at the bank had the bank's security team look at Vandergoat's files and computer records. I understand you two had a nice deal going on, shaking down the orphanage."

Mike continued, "With the pledges and donations we received for running this race, and the reward money for the thugs you sent after me and my team, we will have more than enough money to make the orphanage totally debt free and fund the foundation."

Mister Manhow replied, "You cannot link the men who tried to stop you on the trail to me. I..."

Mike cut him short. "Interesting you said that since no one knows about those men on the trail except you, me, and the State Troopers.

Once I stopped your 'hired guns' on the trail, they all sang like birds about how you paid them to stop me, even to the point of killing the dogs and me. I made a tape of their confessions. I stopped by the State Trooper's office before I finished the race and dropped the tape off. The Troopers did some checking and it seems your "hired guns" have arrest warrants for various crimes in other states. The reward money will go to the orphanage foundation. I guess I should thank you for that. Their confessions on the tape plus the video of you threatening me at my home should put you in jail for a long, long time, my friend."

I could have sworn I heard the man whimper as Mike finished talking to him. Stormy told me that the race officials just stood there dumfounded by Mike's story. As Mike stood up from splinting the man's wrists, one of the race officials asked, "Did you really have amnesia?"

"Yes," Mike replied, "I really did. However, amnesia was not going to stop us from running this race for the orphanage. Fortunately for me, my memory came back a few days after the accident." Mike chuckled as he said, "The hardest part was pretending I still had amnesia after my memory returned. Of course, no one ever asked me if my memory came back. After Mister Manhow and his goons visited my kennel and made their threats, I figured I would use the amnesia to our advantage. Frankly, and fortunately for me, these jerks underestimated us."

I heard a vehicle drive up to the sled. Stormy told me it was a State Trooper vehicle with its flashing lights on.

"Well, Mister Manhow," Mike said, as Stormy told me Mike helped the man get up from the ground. "The party is over. I think these fine peace officers want to give you a ride in their nice shiny truck. Bye."

Stormy told me that the State Troopers talked to Mike and the race officials for a few moments and then took Mister Manhow to their vehicle. After the State Troopers put him inside, they drove off.

I heard Mike walk over to where we were and knell down next to Nitro. Mike said, "I know you wanted a piece of that guy, Nitro, but bad guys taste horrible. Do you want to spoil your appetite for one of Mary's special meals?" Mike continued, "Yep, you guessed it. I got something special to cook up for my team tonight.

Thanks, Team." Stormy told me that Mike put a big hug on Nitro and I sensed Nitro returning to his normal self. Mike gave each of us some TLC. When he was done, he asked the race officials if we were free to go. They told us we were.

I heard Mike zip the sled bag, get on the runners, and pull the sled

hook. "Stand tall, Team. We need to pick up Lakota and get some chow. We had enough fun for today, dealing with 'Iron Dogs' and putting bad dudes in jail. Hike! Hike!" Upon command, we rushed off to find our teammate. Mike started singing a cowboy song. Funny, I really did miss Mike's singing on the trail. You know, I was very happy to hear Christmas say, "Yippee! Our Mike is back and the demons are gone!"

Trail's End

Tundra lead us off the finishing line towards the camping area where we would rest until getting on the plane to go home. We picked up Lakota at the vet clinic. Mike put him the basket. I heard Doctor Jim tell Mike that there was no damage to Lakota's hip. He would be sore for a day or so. Doctor Jim asked Mike to bring Lakota in for a follow-up check and some testing to make sure the cancer continued to stay in check.

We met Randy at the campground and he had a big campfire going. I could feel the nice warmth of the fire. It felt very good after being on the trail. He told Mike that Mary and Caitlyn stayed home to get the house and yard ready for our return. Yes, home, I could picture it in my mind's eye. Just being gone for only a few days makes me long for home.

After Mike and Randy took off our harnesses, they fed us that special meal Mary sent up the trail for us. After chow, we all gathered around the fire to relax and dream. Doctor Jim and Sunny soon joined us. Doctor Jim and Randy were asking Mike questions about our adventures on the trail.

Mike was sitting on the ground. I was on one side of him, while Lakota was lying on Mike's other side. Stormy told me that Lakota had his head on Mike's lap while Mike gave Lakota gentle ear rubs as he talked to Doctor Jim and Randy.

This was so very peaceful. The sounds of the crackling fire. The soft voices of Mike, Randy, and Doctor Jim talking about the race. The snoring of contented dogs. The giggling of the young lady dogs talking young lady dog stuff. The feelings of satisfaction earned from doing a great job and finishing a race for a good cause.

I heard Lakota stand up, "Rivers, I do not feel good."

Before I could bark a word, I heard Mike ask, "Lakota, what is the matter? Why are shaking?"

"Mike!" Doctor Jim said, "Lakota is having a seizure or stroke. Hold on to him very tightly."

"Is that all I can do, just hold him? Is there anything you can do to stop what is happening to him?" Mike pleaded.

Stormy told me that all the dogs were standing up. She told me Mike held Lakota very tight, but Lakota was shaking so bad he shook Mike.

"I am not going to make it. I am getting weaker and cannot breathe. I feel so cold. Oh, I love all of you so much."

Stormy told me Lakota looked right into Mike's face and said. "Thank you Mike. You and Mary gave me a wonderful life. I never knew I could love humans as much as I love you."

Stormy told me Lakota licked Mike's nose and then collapsed onto Mike. I knew Lakota was gone.

I heard Christmas race over to where we were. "No!" she howled, "No."

Home

The flight home was a somber one. No one was barking much. Nitro was trying to comfort Christmas, who was taking Lakota's passing very hard. I knew he could not protect her from the sadness she was feeling. As powerful as Nitro is, I know he felt helpless to comfort Christmas. I gave Nitro a lot of credit for trying, while dealing with his own grief. Lakota was close to all of us.

Normally, when I fly, I doze off, but this time, all I could see in my mind's eye were pictures of Lakota. Our discussions, our travels, his helping me navigate the trails and his courage to protect me. He was my best friend and he told me I was his.

Yes, you may say I was having a very hard time dealing with Lakota leaving us. I hurt and nothing was helping to ease the pain. I heard that time heals all wounds. How I wished time would pass faster so that my hurt would go away.

When we got back to our yard, Stormy told me Mike put Lakota in the warming hut. Lakota was in a plain wooden box Mike obtained in Nome so we could take Lakota home with us. Once we got home, Mike went to his workshop and built a coffin for Lakota. I knew Mike would bury Lakota in our special garden next to Sandy. I was asking Stormy many questions because I wanted to picture all of this in my mind's eye so that I could bury the memories deep inside of me. Gosh, if I could only see!

Stormy told me that Mike carried the coffin from the workshop to the warming hut. He told us to follow him. She told me that the coffin was very beautiful. Stormy walked with me to the warming hut and sat next to me. She told me that all of the dogs, including Stryker and Geezer, were sitting around the table that Mike uses to tend to us or groom us. Lakota was lying on top of the table. Stormy told me he looked so peaceful and handsome. I heard her choke back her tears while I heard Christmas, Sky and Tundra crying.

Stormy said that Mike carefully brushed Lakota's coat and made it

shine. Mike removed Lakota's old green and gold harness and collar, and replaced them with brand new ones. He did not say a word, but Stormy told me his face was wet with tears.

I heard Randy enter the warming hut and say, "Mike, the grave is ready, and so is the sled."

"Thanks Randy, we will be ready in a few minutes." Mike continued, "Please stay here with us until we are ready to go."

Silence, then I heard Mike whisper as Stormy told me that he gave Lakota a big hug. "Lakota, you were a great dog, you took me to Nome and saved my life. You will always be in my heart and mind." Softly, Mike continued, "Thank you, my special buddy, Lakota."

Stormy told me an amazing thing happened next. All the dogs stood up and faced where Lakota was resting. On some silent cue, we all howled our goodbyes to Lakota. When we were done, we all left the warming hut and returned to the yard.

Stormy told me that Randy helped Mike bring Lakota's coffin out of the warming hut and placed it in the basket of our sled. Randy and Mike then harnessed up all of the dogs and put us into our team position. Mike told me I would be a lead dog, along with Christmas. Behind her were Sky, Stormy, and Tundra. Doc told me that he was behind me, followed by Ugly, Brownie, and Nitro, who was in the solo wheel position.

I heard Stryker barking and Christmas told me that he walked over to Mike. Stryker had Lakota's old harness in his mouth. He dropped it at Mike's feet and sat down.

I heard Mike say, "Okay Stryker, you can be in the team for this run."

Mike asked Randy to move Brownie into the vacant wheel position behind Tundra. Mike harnessed up Stryker and hooked him onto the gang line between Nitro and Ugly. I heard the door of the big house open. Christmas told me Mary and Caitlyn, with Geezer in his special harness for guiding Caitlyn, came into the yard to join us. We will give Lakota his final sled ride, together, as a team and, as his family.

We did not run to the special garden, we walked very slowly, as if we did not want this run to end. Once there, Christmas told me that Mike and Randy lifted Lakota's coffin off the sled and gently placed it into the open grave. Mike's voice trembled as he said, "Lakota, thank you for being a part of my life and for protecting me. You are a true champion. Come Spring, we will plant flowers and dress up your gravesite as we did for Sandy. Run with Sandy, Lakota, and be free of the limitations of your body. Bye, Lakota, I love you."

Mary, Randy, and Caitlyn also said some nice things about Lakota. When they were finished, Mike took Christmas and me off the gang line and asked Randy to take the team back to the yard. As I heard the team walk away, Mike let us sit for a while by Lakota's grave.

"Rivers, I know you and Lakota were together for a long time. Christmas, I suspect that Lakota protected you when you and he were lost." Mike continued, "I figured you would like to join me in some quite time with him right now." We sat there, together, while Mike gave us gentle ear rubs.

When we returned to the yard, Mike helped me to my doghouse. I was sad. Lakota died so quickly that I did not even get to say good-bye to him while he was alive. I was not a happy Husky and I guess it showed to the rest of my teammates. I was a bit short with them when they tried to comfort me.

"Uncle Rivers, you want to go for a walk?" Stormy asked.

"No," I said curtly.

"Uncle Rivers, will you tell us the story of the Rainbow Bridge?" Tundra and Sky asked.

"No, leave me alone," I replied.

I heard Christmas come to the front of my doghouse and ask, "Uncle Rivers, why were you so short with my girls? All they wanted to do was help you feel better." Before I could answer her, she continued, "Uncle Rivers, I am so disappointed with you."

"And so am I, Mister Rivers." I know that voice. It was Sandy! I jumped out of my doghouse and I saw her. Remember, she gives me the gift of sight every time she visits me. She was sitting there, next to Christmas and her girls. I felt a paw touch me. When I turned around to see who touched me, I saw the rest of the team sitting all around me. I looked into each of their faces. They were all smiling! How can they be happy at a time like this? Lakota is gone.

"Rivers, I think you and I need to take a walk." I know that voice. I turned towards the voice and saw Lakota. I was barkless. Lakota was a young dog. His coat shined so much it looked as if it glowed. His eyes were clear and his voice was strong and powerful. He wore a beautiful golden harness with glowing green streaks woven through it. Our team colors! The diamonds on his harness were brighter than any star in the sky. His collar matched the harness.

"Come with me, Rivers," Lakota said as he nudged me to walk with him, away from the group. We walked in silence stopping by the spot

111

by the back fence where I heard Christmas crying on that Christmas Eve a long time ago.

"Rivers, you need to stop feeling sad and get on with your life," Lakota said.

"It is hard, Lakota. I miss you so much. I find it difficult to accept that you died," I replied.

"Rivers, you think too hard and sometimes not about the right stuff," Lakota said gently. "I was a very old dog in a very used body. My heart was weak. It was only a matter of time before I would die. But you, Rivers, you did a great thing that saved Mike's life."

"And what was that?" I asked.

"Remember when we were on the last part of the trail to Nome and I told you I could not make it?" Lakota asked. I nodded as Lakota continued, "You told me to stop being stubborn and ride in the basket to Nome. If you did not do that, I would have died before we reached Nome. I would not have been in the basket to save Mike when that dude went after him with the baseball bat. Rivers, I died with my friends and my family around me. I saved my human. I died with no pain and very peacefully in the arms of my beloved human. Can a Husky ask for anything more than that?"

Lakota continued, "Rivers, we are only here for a short time. During our short lives, we have to accomplish so much while dealing with our own challenges. Once our job here is finished, we leave this life and move on."

"Rivers, look at me," Lakota said. "Do you see a tired old dog who battled cancer, or a young, healthy dog, full of life? Look into my eyes, they are clear, and they sparkle." Lakota continued, "How can you feel so sad when I am in a better place, a place where you will join me when your job here is finished. Rivers, think about this for a second. You will be able to see when you join me!"

"But I miss you now, Lakota. I miss talking to you and running the trails with you," I said.

"Rivers," Lakota replied. "How can you miss me when I am in your heart and memories? Believe me, Rivers, in time we will be together again, racing over trails of perfect snow, and running so fast that we will streak across the sky like shooting stars!"

Silence for a moment, then, Lakota said, "Good, I am glad you are thinking about it. Now, we need to return to the team. I need to talk to them."

"Lakota," I said as I started to feel better. "Thank you."

"No, Rivers, thank you," Lakota replied. "If you did not share your biscuits with me the first time you met Mike, he would never have become my human, and I would never have enjoyed the great life I had here with Mike, Mary, you and my other teammates. If it were not for your random act of kindness with those biscuits, I would not have been there to save Christmas when she and I were lost. Rivers, you helped me to fulfill my Husky heritage, just as you have helped so many others. And Rivers, even though I am not physically here with you, you still are, and always will be, my best friend."

As we rejoined the group, I felt much better. I was actually happy now that I realized my best friend is still with me, looking out for me, and free of, as Mike said, the limitations of his body.

"Okay, I need to get back soon," Lakota said to the other dogs in the yard. "But I want to tell you a few things before I go. Please do not feel sad that I have left you. I am with you in your hearts and memories. I am looking out for you, and guiding you on your trails. As I told Rivers, we all will be together again racing, over perfect trails with the Northern Lights dancing all around us."

Lakota continued, "The stories you heard about crossing the Rainbow Bridge are very true. There are no sick dogs, no blind dogs, no deaf dogs, and no lame dogs. All dogs are young, healthy, happy, and stay that way forever. We wait for our beloved humans to cross the Bridge and be with us."

Christmas asked, "Uncle Lakota, why are you wearing that beautiful golden harness with glowing green streaks and diamonds on it? Aunt Sandy's collar is the same color. I thought all dogs who cross the Bridge wore silver harnesses or collars."

Lakota answered, "Yes, 'Little One' what you say is true. Working dogs wear a silver harness and all dogs receive a silver collar." Lakota continued, "However, if a dog protected his human from harm, then that dog earned the golden harness with diamonds or the golden collar with diamonds. If they are part a team, like Sandy and I were, the team's colors are woven into our harness and collars."

Sandy said, "I earned my golden collar when I protected Mike from the two dogs that tried to attack him when Rivers stayed with us in the city. Lakota earned his several times starting with protecting Missy from the bear when you all first moved here."

"Actually," Lakota added, "You all have earned golden harness or collars. Geezer, Doc, Brownie, Christmas, Sky, Stormy, and Ugly

earned theirs when they protected Caitlyn from the wild dogs. Tundra earned hers when she took out the "Iron Dog" driver who tried to run over Mike. Stryker earned his protecting his human in the war zone. Nitro earned his when he protected Mike from the dude with the knife at the end of Randy's first race. And, Rivers, my dear friend, you have one also. You earned it when you jumped up and protected Mike from that guy with the knife."

"Sandy and I must go," Lakota said. "I will not say goodbye because goodbye is a forever thing. I will say so long for now, because you all will be joining Sandy and me when it is your time to cross the Bridge. In the meantime, remember your Husky heritage. Protect and love your humans. They need you."

They were gone, but I had a few fast seconds of sight left to look at my teammates. They all had happy faces. Each one, including me, was at peace with Lakota's passing. Thank you, Sandy, for this gift, also.

Afterthoughts

Mike once said that, to him, if life is not an adventure, then it is just one long boring existence. Awhile after returning home from Nome, I sat in my favorite corner of the yard. I was thinking about my life before meeting Mike. Now, I realized that what I experienced before was just an existence. After "adopting" Mike, my life has become one great adventure after another.

The video tape of Mister Manhow's threats and the confessions of his 'Iron Dog' drivers sent them to prison. They will not be around to bother us in our lifetimes, or Randy's or Caitlyn's. Mister Vandergoat lost his job. Mike told us that Mister Vandergoat's actions did not result in jail time for him. However, Mike told us that it would be a long time before any banks hire him. Rumor has it that Mister Vandergoat was "asked" to leave Alaska. I bet he did.

I take a lot of comfort in remembering Lakota's words He once told me he realized he must live each day to its fullest. It could be his last. How true, I thought. We have only a short time to spend with our humans and let them feel our unconditional love for them. When we leave them to cross the Bridge, our humans grieve for us. I just hope they take comfort in the love we gave them. Yes, I do miss Lakota, but I know he is one happy Husky these days, and each day, I cherish the vivid thoughts and memories I have of my best friend.

The rebuilt orphanage was so much better than the original building. Mike said it was a "state of the art" home with a high-tech learning center. I heard him mutter something about "grooming the children for success with knowledge." I understand he had a hand in designing the building and monitored the construction. During the rebuilding, Mike would take Caitlyn and me over to the building site. Mike would describe the building to both of us. Caitlyn would ask many questions. She also gave Mike and the builders many ideas as to what the new orphanage needed besides being a home full of TLC for the needy children.

Stormy told me that the orphanage is a beautiful home-type build-

ing. Mrs. Astor was very proud of her new building and gave us a tour of it. Yes, she let all of us dogs wander through it. Okay, I cannot see it, but Stormy described everything to me, so my mind's eye created a great picture of what it looks like.

Mary said it was very homey with the bedrooms shared by only two children. It was not an open bay style dorm, Mike added. The children named each bedroom after a dog on our team or in our home. Stormy told me the color of the "Sky" and "Christmas" rooms were icy blue, the same color as Christmas and Sky's eyes.

The "Tundra Room" was the color of tennis balls. Very appropriate, I thought. However, what is the color of a tennis ball? I played with them, but never really saw them. Tunny said it looked like a fun room to live in.

Stormy said her room, the "Stormy Room", was a gold color that matched her eyes. Stormy has golden colored eyes? I never knew that. Stormy told me that the "Rivers Room" had the most windows and those windows overlooked the trail that we travel on from our home to the orphanage. I bet if I lived here and could see, I would sit all day by the windows and look out of them, waiting for my team to visit.

I asked Stormy where the "Lakota Room" was. She led me downstairs to the main floor. "Uncle Rivers, Uncle Lakota does not have a bedroom here. The 'Lakota Room' is the library!" How fitting I thought, a room where you can gain knowledge and think. Yes, remember Lakota was a thinker. I smiled, knowing that Lakota would be very happy to have the library named after him. Stormy told me that there was a great picture of Lakota on the wall.

Not surprisingly, the children named the kitchen and dining room after Mary. Hmm, "Mary's House of Chow," I wondered. Rumor was that the all the children put on weight at our place during their stay. I told you Mary's chow was good stuff.

There are two, "big-stuffed Huskies" for cuddling in each of the girls' rooms. The boys' rooms have big pictures of them working with the team when they were our "dog handlers." Mike commented that the orphanage looked and felt more like a loving home than an institution. Yes, it sounded like a very nice home for our friends at the orphanage. It made me feel good that I had a part in making it so.

When I was finished thinking and remembering, I stood up walk back to join the other dogs in the yard. Before I could take a few paw steps, Stormy was right by my side, acting as my "eyes."

"Stormy," I asked. "Where is Tunny?"

"She is sitting with momma Christmas," Stormy replied. "Do you want me to walk with you to her, Uncle Rivers"?

"Please do," I replied.

"Hi Uncle Rivers," Christmas said. "How are you doing today?"

"Fine, Christmas," I replied. "Would you mind if Tunny and I take a short walk?"

"Of course not, Uncle Rivers." Christmas said, "Tunny, how about taking a walk with your Uncle Rivers."

I heard Tundra stand up and move closer to me. "Sure thing. Where are we going, Uncle Rivers?" she asked.

"Would you mind walking with me to my doghouse, Tunny?" I asked as we started our walk. "Tunny, you did a great job on the trail during the race. Knocking that driver off the 'Iron Dog' like you did saved Mike's life, as well as the rest of the team," I told her.

"You and the other dogs would have done the same thing. It is our Husky heritage to protect our musher, our human," Tunny said. I noticed a tone of humility in her bark. Yes, Tunny was maturing.

"Doc told me that when you two led the team into Nome, you were in fact the lead dog. Doc told your uncles that he laid back and let you lead the team across the finish line," I told her. "He said you did an excellent job, and you are a superb credit to your Husky heritage. Doc is very proud of you."

We stopped walking as we reached my doghouse. "Did Uncle Doc really say those things about me, Uncle Rivers? You are not pulling my tail, are you?"

"No, Tunny, I would not do that to you. The fact is, Tunny, all of your uncles think you did a super job. You made all of us very proud of you," I said.

I continued, "I saw Aunt Sandy by your side after you took out the 'Iron Dog' driver. I know you made her very proud also."

"You saw Aunt Sandy?" Tunny asked.

"Yes," I replied. "She gave me the gift of sight whenever she comes to visit." I continued, "I know she has given you some gifts also. The big one being courage. Chasing down that 'Iron Dog' and then taking out the driver the way you did took a great deal of courage and fast thinking."

Silence. It was a bit unusual for Tunny not to have something to bark about.

"So, after all of the good things you did, leading the team, saving Mike's life, making all of us very proud of you, do you still believe that you are a 'no-good dog'?" I asked.

No reply.

I asked her, "Did you hear Mike tell the race official at the finish line that he had to fake losing his memory after it came back? I know it bothered him to let you feel so bad because you blamed yourself for what happen to him." I continued, "I think it is time for Mike to stop feeling bad about what he had to do. I know you can help him feel better."

"How?" Tunny asked.

I stuck my head into my doghouse, grabbed several of Tunny's tennis balls, and dropped them on the ground by her paws. "You can take one of these tennis balls and get Mike to play 'Fetch' with you," I said.

"My tennis balls!" Tunny exclaimed. "Where did you get them, Uncle Rivers?"

"I dug them up and saved them for you. I knew you would need and want them."

"Do you think Mike would play with me?" Tundra asked.

"What do you think?" I replied.

Almost as if on cue, I heard Mike come into the kennel as Christmas walked over to where Tundra and I were standing. Christmas told me that Tundra picked up a tennis ball and raced to where Mike was. Tundra dropped the tennis ball by Mike's feet. Then she started to "talk" to him, while "dancing" all around him. Mike started to laugh as he picked up the tennis ball and threw it. They started playing the "Fetch" game just as they did before the race. Super, I thought.

"It looks like Tunny is back to her old self," I heard Lakota whispering to me. I could picture his smiling face watching over us.

"Yep," I whispered, "I guess everything actually does happen for the best."

See Ya

Acknowledgements

I am very fortunate to have friends who helped me write the Rivers series of books. While the stories "mushed" around in my head, the following people helped me to get the pictures in my "mind's eye" onto paper for you to read. The story telling was the easy part; it took friends to get the stories into print.

Doctor James Gaarder: Besides being a great friend to both Rivers and myself, Doctor Jim allowed me to use his "persona" for my Doctor Jim character. I sincerely hope that his caring and skill has manifested itself in my portrayal of him. Doctor Jim also helped me with the technical aspects of my books. However, most importantly, Doctor Jim made Rivers pain free.

Thank you, Doctor Jim.

The Wasilla Vet Clinic: The clinic provided and continues to provide the day-to-day care of our dogs. The professional staff of the Wasilla Vet clinic doctored Rivers' fat mass on his hip, Lakota's cancer, and bad paws, plus Tundra's detached fang and bit ear, as well as the yearly check-ups and shots for the team.

Thank you, Staff of the Wasilla Vet Clinic.

Test Readers Team: "Brookie Cookie," Tajana, Evva, Sandy, Katie, and Rosemary were my test readers. They did an excellent job "giving it to me straight." Their job was not easy because all of them are Rivers fans and could tend to be biased. Sandy and Rosemary have used Rivers' books in their classes. All have given Rivers ear rubs except Rosemary, who has not ventured to Alaska yet.

Thank you Test Reader Team!

Tajana   *Katie with her*   *Brookie Cookie,*   *Evva with Mike*
and Rivers   *horse Funny Face*   *with Rivers*   *and Rivers*
                                      and Lakota

Proof Reading Team: Robyn of "Marriart," Donna of Husky Productions, and GG of Anchorage were my proofreaders. They "volunteered" for the difficult task of wading thru my New York-esse and ensuring it conformed somewhat to the "Queen's English." Robyn, my former co-worker and dear friend, is an artist specializing in glass-fusion art pieces. Donna's passion is filmmaking and Huskies. GG is a former teacher and Husky lover. All have strong backgrounds in editing and proofing. They accepted the concept that to write a dog story from the dog's point of view, you have to think like a dog. Since dogs do not think like humans, you may find a stray punctuation mark, or dangling modifier. Therefore, if you find a "gotcha" just keep in mind that to err is human, to forgive is canine!
Thank you, Robyn, Donna, and GG.

Rivers: I tell people that Rivers "adopted" me in 2000. What I do not tell many people is that Rivers has been a tremendous inspiration to me and changed my life for the good. I have watched him transform from a lonely kennel dog to a loving, funny, and obedient companion

 dog. I have watched him "learn" things as an adult dog he should have learned as a puppy. When Icy (Christmas in our books) and Lakota were lost for 9 days in 2002, Rivers played the "adopted parent" for Icy's puppies, caring for them until we found Icy and Lakota. Even today, he licks the puppies' faces when they get upset at him if he accidently steps on one of them. The puppies, Tundra, Stormy, and Sky are 5 years old as of August 2007. While they

are bigger than Rivers, they show him a great deal of respect and consideration for his challenge, being blind. They demonstrate what "showing respect for your elders" really means. Simply stated, Rivers is their leader. *Thank you, Rivers,* for motivating me to be the human you trusted me to be.

Lakota: Lakota typified the "strong and silent" type, and boy, did he have a beautiful howl! Lakota was a very unpretentious and appreciative dog. He, like Rivers, was a kennel dog who made the transition into a great companion dog. La-  kota was a cancer survivor. After giving up a kidney to cancer, Lakota acted like a dog half his age, living his life to the fullest. He loved playing with Icy and at times, they were inseparable. We sincerely believed that Lakota took care of Icy when they were lost. In turn, she "mothered" him when he was sick. Icy was 8 years his junior. As an old warrior, Lakota continued to "protect" his kennel, but he relinquished most of the barking to the younger dogs. Lakota showed me his patience, caring, and thirst for life. You, like Rivers, inspired me to be the human you knew I was. I miss you Buddy.

Thank you, Lakota.

I need to thank the other dogs I wrote about in these stories. Most are dogs I knew or worked with. Icy, Sky, Stormy, and Tundra live with us, along with Rivers, Sandy, and Lakota. They all have provided inspirations for parts of this book. Nitro, Doc, Ugly, Brownie, and Fin live with other friends. Sunny is the only dog character not actually based upon a dog. The basis for the Sunny dog character was a student of mine, a heroic, beautiful person who died when she succumbed to the intense challenges of her life.

Thank you, Team!

Mary, my wife: From the very beginning of this adventure in 2000 (the adventure was really her idea) through this book, the books signings, the late meetings, the book sales, the meals on the run, and

the many "paw chores" she does, Mary has been there for me, giving me "space to create". They say that behind every great man is a great woman. Well, I do not consider myself great (good is also questionable), but Mary is truly a great person. Writing these books without you would have been impossible.

Thank you, thank you very much, Mary.

Thank you all,

Mike Dillingham

Side Trails

As Rivers "barked" in our second book, *Rivers Through the Eyes of a Blind Dog*, some of the adventures and characters in this book are, well "tales of the trails, from wagging tails", as seen through the eyes of a blind dog.

Sunny (real name Chena) and Fin (real name Sissy) on the Cast of Critters pages were Donna's beloved companion dogs. Sissy and Chena are waiting for Donna on the other side of the Rainbow Bridge. **Donna Quante, of Husky Productions,** donated their pictures to this book.

Bernadette Anne donated the picture of her Benjamin (Geezer in this book), from her private collection. Benjamin lived the second half of his life with Bernadette, after he fought his battle with jaw cancer and won. We know that Benjamin is waiting for Bernadette across the Rainbow Bridge

Ronald L. Aiello, President of the United States War Dog Association, donated the picture we used for Stryker. The dog's real name was Stormy. Stormy was a US War Dog and Ron was her handler in Viet Nam. According to Ron, Stormy saved his life many times. This is a picture of Ron and Stormy in Viet Nam sometime between 1966 and 1967. Stormy did not come home from Vietnam. She is waiting for Ron on the other side of the Rainbow Bridge. Please visit the US War Dog association web site at: http://uswardogs.org/index.html.

Contacting Rivers

Rivers attempts to answer all e-mail he receives. E-mail at either: Rivers@rogershsa.com or Riversbooks@gmail.com for his free e-mail newsletter.

Rivers' Blog is located at: http://www.riversbooks.blogspot.com

To order Rivers' books, please go to: http://orderriversbooks. blogspot.com/

Rivers' website is located at: http://home.gci.net/~sleddog

Rivers' mailing address is:
Rivers
% Rivers Books
PO Box 876308
Wasilla, Alaska 99687-6308